GW00467986

J. J. Cole

RAPTUROUS MEN

Vanguard Press

A CIP catalogue record for this title is
available from the British Library.

ISBN 978-1-80016-162-7

*Vanguard Press is an imprint of
Pegasus Elliot MacKenzie Publishers Ltd.*
www.pegasuspublishers.com

First Published in 2021

**Vanguard Press
Sheraton House Castle Park
Cambridge England**

Printed & Bound in Great Britain

About the author

J.J. Coleman is a fiction writer from the hearty town of Dover, overlooking the captivating English Channel. He was educated at a Catholic school and from an early age developed a sweet tooth for literature and genre works. Shakespeare, Lovecraft, Dante, Grimm Brothers, Dickens, Chaucer, Milton, Richard Adams and a host of others have all played a part in Jamie's inspirations. In a hobby that has been steadily nurtured throughout his youth, Jamie's passion for writing steadily grew and has led to this publication.

RAPTUROUS MEN

Dedication

To He who conjures all things, including this — this is
for you

At the back of the Milne warehouse in the heart of the Sparks borough, they were encouraged to look upon the bodies as they wasted away with flies and maggots ravaging around them. "Look at them, this is what he does, this is what you're up against!" he warns them.

On the ground beneath them were some twenty bodies, all of which displayed signs of extreme torture and severe trauma; some even displaying signs of sexual assault, and one man was responsible for it all. It was this one man, this beast, who served as the catalyst for such a gathering, the notorious mass murderer. Long John. For some forty years he had terrorised the people of the Sparks borough with senseless and unjustified violence which led to the appalling murders of many hundreds; it is only the death of a particular individual that has led the Mayor in particular to act. Before then, modest bounties were bestowed by businessmen who could afford it. But now he had been forced into action, now knowing the effects first hand as to the horror that besieged this place.

Amongst the pile of rotting innocents laid Maria, the Mayor's daughter, a beautiful woman with respectable credentials who had barely reached adulthood. He wept as he told the men of the infamous

Long John though most of them had already heard the gruesome stories attributed to him; a violent fiend who attacked without justification against any he wished. He killed indiscriminately and saw the likes of women, children and the elderly as no exceptions. The majority of the men had heard the tales of Long John's actions where he has torn innocents to pieces with his bare hands and made decorative displays from the remains, they had also heard of his immense height and sickening smile that was permanently visible. A nightmarish view to match the hideous action.

Long John was certainly a violent man, but these men who stood before the weeping Mayor were no strangers to violence for it was a daily occurrence in their lives. That was why they were there after all. Amongst these men were criminals, gangsters and bounty hunters from an array of organised crime syndicates — professionals of their craft, monsters to most but perhaps the saviours long awaited. The Mayor was entrusting these strangers to finally rid the Sparks borough of this murderous darkness and to establish the light of peace that once lived.

Overlooking the besieged bodies from a respectable distance were Gerald Daniels, Piper Vauss and Abijah Gordan. The trio were known as the Coffin Bearers for their investment and storing of ill-gotten gains into morgues and funeral stores. They were undertakers by trade but made their riches in turf wars, drugs, prostitution and the selling of arms amongst a host of others. They were based in the boroughs to the north and had come down to Sparks especially for this. Gerald was the head of the spear in this syndicate and had entrusted Piper (his number two) and Abijah (a renowned brute) to accompany him. His posse was less than a fraction to the army of devotees available to him, but he needed his very best for this and them alone.

Standing to their left were Jensen, James and Jakub Turner. Known as the Turner Triplets, these three were sneaky fighters who often spoke with words far bigger than their physical sizes should have allowed them. They ran a host of boxing rings and rigged betting odds to ensure maximum profits. Growing up in prolific poverty in London's east, these men now lived undisciplined lives in wealth and leisure. But they were respected immensely in the land they made their own and had many powerful contacts as a result. Contacts that would often go to them should a certain individual need silencing. But for them, that would be on hold for now. Like the Coffin Bearers, the midget triplets dropped their current affairs in pursuit of a price tag that was simply too large to refuse.

Standing to their left was Charles Black and his posse: Brodie, Karl, Ace, Quentin, Jeffrey and Michael. Known as Cyrenius' Westerners, these seven men were sent on behalf of the infamous Cyrenius the Cowboy from the fantasy Wild West. Cowboys by nature, these men were animals and were renowned for their activities in that dust bowl. Their victims couldn't be counted, and they had besieged hundreds of thousands from the disorganised governments which often revered them as heroes amongst many. But whilst some saw them as heroes, to many more they were brutal thugs who tortured and gruesomely maimed any who fell foul to them or tried to mingle with their affairs. Charles was Cyrenius' number two and personally known for brutally killing four armed men with nothing but a club. His presence made sense though all others wished otherwise.

To their left was the London Raj led by Balteg Reddy, sticking out like a sore thumb. Accompanying him were his best enforcers: Attamjit, Deenpal and Gopal. They were a Sikh organised crime syndicate stationed in the northern boroughs, right next to the Coffin Bearers. They stood out with their brazen and extravagant turbans such as the very ones they donned now. Bright and dazzling. Neighbours all respected the boundaries mutually agreed between Balteg and Gerald, and their presence here would signify the two groups' first gathering in a long time. Balteg wore his signature white turban which held a perfectly cut ruby at its centre, reflecting bright in the sun's rays, and he was first to be noticed by all. Balteg and his men traded in horses and general livestock, often disguising sick animals as healthy purebreds to maximise profits. But it should be said they were no strangers to conflict, and known for the vicious and torturous art of scalping, which in turn, had given them a reputation for prolonging the deaths of those they captured.

To their left was Gerald's arch-rival, Helmswood. They were rival undertakers who also specialised in the funeral trade and were led by the precarious Abel Rees. Accompanying him were his most loyal men: Benjamin, Jude, Eli and Nathan. Faces Gerald and his guys knew all too well. Although they were based in the south, they often came into conflict with Gerald and his Coffin Bearers and uncountable conflicts had arisen as a consequence, which led to the tortures and murders of dozens on both sides. Seeing one another in such a confined space proved difficult for the pair of them — the blood spilt from their last encounter barely dry, but this was no time for a war between men. So, with the greatest of restraints, both sides did their best to ignore the other.

Towards their left was the infamous Los Hijos Sangrientos or The Bloody Sons. A blood-stained syndicate based in Ciudad Juarez who rose to notoriety after the killing of Buddha Patel just three years earlier. Easily recognisable by their tribal markings covering

13

their faces and arms, such a killing easily made them one of the most recognisable groups present, but that wouldn't necessarily be a bonus for them. They traded in a host of narcotics, along with slaves, and emerged as the alpha syndicate of the Mexican city after torturing all of their rivals into submission, often with that infamous killing striking fear strong enough to cause voluntary surrender. Their history and current status perhaps made them the most suitable for this action in their eyes, evident by their brazen grins. But such fools would do well to remember that this was no Buddha Patel and it was a far cry from the safety of their blood-soaked sands. The group's number three, Jose Lopez, was representing their interests here and was accompanied by a trusted inner circle comprised of Alejandro, Jorge, Arturo, Juan, Raul and Rafael.

And finally, to their left stood a lone man, with notoriety far superior to all the others combined. Stanley Taylor. He had no syndicate and no allegiance to anyone other than himself, a one-man army as it were, whose reputation has rendered him by reservists as one of the most dangerous men in the world especially among fanatics. Unlike the others, he specialised in the art that was bounty hunting and had done so long before the hairs began to spring from his chest. This behemoth had killed beyond what can be known, with many of his victims being notorious murderers who had special gifts like Long John. There he stood, alone with his black frock coat and top hat with a black mask that depicted something of Aztec inspiration. He rarely ever spoke, but then again, his reputation ensured he didn't need to.

These thirty-two men, comprised of different syndicates and allegiances, were being entrusted by the Mayor to kill a man who many claimed to be invincible They would serve as a systematic effort to eliminate a man that strikes fear into the hearts of the bravest when nothing more than his name is mentioned.

"I have got eighty-five thousand pounds for person or persons who bring me back the head of this devil incarnate!" the Mayor shouted emotionally. "The reputations you carry are well seeded but that all means nothing here. Long John cares not for who you are or what you've done. He sees you as all the same. Cockroaches, easily squishable."

The cocksure members of the Bloody Sons laughed with its leader unapologetically responding, "Clearly you need reminding that we slayed, Buddha Patel. A half man, half hog with fifty stone of weight. Many had come before us and could not vanquish him, but we did, and history will repeat itself here!" said Jose. An outward display of cultish euphoria commenced within the ranks of the Bloody Sons as their leading representative spoke his words of certainty — singing with Spanish tone and dancing in a peculiar manner.

It was during this that Gerald leaned back and spoke into the ear of Abijah, who stood close behind. "Clearly, he hasn't met you."

Abijah sighed, knowing his boss' words were true, but was quick to lock eyes with a certain pair as they came into mind soon after. He looked over to Charles Black of the Cyrenius' Westerners and then to Stanley Taylor. The pair had conjured the same thought sooner and were already gazing across to Abijah. Thus, a triangle of the sharpest stares commenced, each of them more concerned with the opposing pair than with any of the inferiors that surrounded them. They knew, logically and realistically, that it was only one of them that stood a chance at savaging the beast. They were taller than the others and were built in a way that rendered them uniquely strong; stronger and more resilient than any normal man. Abijah was 6'6, Charles 6'5 and Stanley 6'7. They were built like horses which often resulted in people of their calibre being known as such. "Horsemen," they were dubbed. A breed of uniquely strong men who were seen as perfect rivals for those known as "Greats"— those like Long John. Such men were rare and of high asset, and to find one in a crowd of six figures was special. Forever more this would be, as three stood in a crowd of less than thirty. Eventually, they ceased their staring and focussed on the tribal Hispanics who foolishly fancied themselves. None of the three ever saw this "Buddha Patel" nor had the rest, but all were certain he was not of the same breed as Long John. A fact, these naïve specimens would undoubtedly find out sooner or later.

The Mayor grew visibly angry, seeing the group's false certainty, and displayed a tearful outburst. "You're so brazen now, but you won't be when you see him!" he shouted in a manner with such grief that the hideous dancing soon froze and the smiles would no longer grow. "Long John is no mere man, he is a fiend of monstrous proportions who is capable of tearing you limb from limb with not a sweat or grunt!" The Mayor then searched the space with his piercing gaze and was quick to notice that the foolishness had spread, seeing that The Triplets and the Sikhs were smiling in the absence of seriousness.

When they saw his glance, they too surrendered foolish thoughts, but even that wouldn't prevent the Mayor's words to follow. "You think you are the first? You think you are special?" he shouted. "Many have come, fancying themselves unique and brave with reputations they think hold value, but have all ended up the same — torn to pieces if they're lucky, or become part of his hideous displays. He is a monster, unlike anything any of you have seen or ever will. I know you are here for the money and those who kill him will certainly get it, but I implore you to be motivated by something other than this. You're going to need it if you want to end his reign of terror."

It was at this moment that the originally rapturous men were no longer so certain of themselves and were beginning to realise the calibre of opponent they would be facing. Not a word nor smile was to follow as the Mayor departed, leaving them to stare at those horrifically mangled bodies before them.

The sharpness of the moon protruding from thick cloud had come to the streets of Sparks borough, which would now fall mostly silent with barely a soul in sight, creating an eerie atmosphere which the sounds of drifting rubbish and squeaks of rats would mainly dominate.

"How dull is such a place, one would be forgiven for thinking this wasn't even London," said Piper, unimpressed by the scenery as they walked its pavements.

"Rubbish and rats. It's certainly London," replied Gerald. "It's just as I expected. Desolate and dark, with a beast of a man lurking within." Gerald's last words resonated in Abijah's mind as he walked closely behind him and Piper, anticipating the sight of such a fiend.

As the trio of men walked the largely desolate and ill-kept streets, they noticed the only source of light amongst the thick darkness, that from a pub in the distance, to their right, standing out tremendously.

There wasn't to be a word or degree of hesitation as they headed in its direction. Famished and parched, they were impatient for what awaited them at the hotel.

They entered the pub and the few faces it harboured turned towards them with an eerie silence to match the lifeless atmosphere. Gerald and his trusted posse said nothing as they focussed on every face in the room. Staring at each face intensively, making their presence known. Gerald and the others then walked to one of the many empty tables, heading for one away from windows and positioned in the corner. The table was darkened, for the dwindling light could hardly reach that far; the perfect table to avoid attention. They sat and hardly had a second to pull in their chairs before the barman came to them, delivering them unordered booze and hastily moving without payment. The three sipped whilst maintaining eyes on every pair in the room. Eight in all, scattered throughout.

Thunder and lightning soon followed and with it the harsh sprays of nature against the structure that shielded them, adding to the intensity of the room. They watched on in silence as most eyes in the room attempted to discreetly glare in their direction. Clearly, their presence wasn't welcome. Their statures imitated one another, one hand on the glass and the other hovering around their concealed defences, strapped between belt and buckle. The wall was all that viewed their backs, their attention focussed fully forward. One sudden move from the onlookers and the pub would not be so eerie.

A man entered the pub and gazed across its interior with no apology. He saw Gerald and the others sitting at the table in the far corner before scarpering back outside with natural effort. Piper, ensuring he wasn't the only one to notice this, went to inform Gerald:

"Gerald, did you s—" he said before being interrupted by a simple:

"Saw it," by Gerald. None of the three were fools, they had been in this game for too long. They had become familiar with specific behaviours for they had employed such tactics themselves, so all would have noticed the poor subtlety of the young gent as he vacated the pub the moment Gerald's face met with his. Grips were tight around their glasses, almost tight enough to shatter, but there would be no more sipping from here.

Moments later, a group of six men entered the pub. Among them, the man seen gazing just moments before. All came in with purpose, though it was one that widened the trio's eyes. The man who led with the others, their old rival, Timothy Palmer. None of the three could've guessed that such a day would harbour any more surprises, and yet here was a stifling one. The Coffin Bearers knew Timothy had moved south, but fell just short of a heart attack once Gerald saw his mug here of all places. Not from fear, but of bewildering bad luck. Such a presence could make a mud situation even muddier. But just how muddy, he and the others would wonder, a notion they were about to find out.

It took less than a second for Gerald and Timothy's eyes to lock, followed immediately by the latter's sharp approach to the table.

"Boss?" asks Abijah, his hand firmly on his belt.

"It's fine," Gerald muttered to him and Viper, as he was seated between them.

Timothy's people would keep a distance, standing in a distanced line before the table, whilst Timothy himself grabbed a chair from the neighbouring table and sat at the side of theirs. Gerald looked at him with a stern face whilst Abijah and Piper remained still and motionless. As Gerald looked at Timothy, he couldn't help but notice the few punters in the background were now gone, even the barman.

"Daniels" said Timothy.

"Palmer," Gerald responded.

The pair stared at one another in what was a tense and unpredictable situation, neither knowing what the other was thinking, but imagining all likely outcomes nonetheless.

"I knew I'd find you here," Timothy eventually said. "In my fucking borough."

Gerald sighed. "Yeah, and how's that?" he asked.

Timothy leant in close and whilst Abijah's grip around his belt couldn't be any tighter.

"Well, it was quite simple really. First, I hear that the Mayor put a huge bounty on the head of Long John and then I get reports of fucking small-time syndicates entering my borough from all over the fucking joint! And when they said some were coming from the north, well, it couldn't really be anybody else could it?"

Gerald looked at Timothy and exhaled deeply through his nose before replying. "And I suppose you want us to leave now, is that it?"

Timothy displayed an exaggerated smile and nodded in a sarcastic manner for the answer was obvious, but Gerald remained still and found an error in Timothy's position that had to be questioned.

"Before this conversation turns physical, I do have one question," said Gerald.

Timothy leant back and opened his arms as if goading him to ask. Gerald continued, "Why do you want Long John kept alive?"

Timothy sniggered as he replied, "Long John has been here for forty years, so let's not talk as if you will be the one to end him. He can't be killed and I don't want the likes of your kind turning my borough into a bloodbath just to prove it. Besides, he tears my challengers to shreds and I don't even have to pay for the privilege."

"Well, that will end soon," said Gerald as he looked across the table at Abijah.

Timothy laughed and shouted, "You always were a brave wanker, but foolish too," before leaning in close once more. "It won't just be me you'll piss off by going after him. The people will not be happy," Timothy continued. "You see, Long John is what many here see as a... necessary evil. Sure, he tears innocents to shreds from time to time but his presence often keeps Sparks free from the wretched gangland and turf wars that plague everywhere else in London."

"Can't be entirely the case, as you are here, after all," Piper said freely.

Timothy displayed a light grin with the heaviest demeanour as he responded, "We work around him, not against him. Hell, many on these streets even walk beside him, not so much as batting an eyelid."

What Timothy said highlighted a social divide in Sparks, a divide between those who wanted Long John vanquished and others who viewed him as a necessary evil who kept them safe from an even worse alternative. Whilst Timothy and his posse were active in the borough, there were no rivals to create a conflict as most syndicates and clans would not step foot in Sparks. Killing Long John, or even attempting to, would not be received well by many of the populace. But this was far from a surprise to Gerald. Stories of Long John had reached far beyond Sparks. That, and the sympathies the people here had towards him.

Gerald laughed as he picked up his glass and drank greatly from it, "Now if I cared what people thought of me, then I would've packed up and ran down south like a bitch. Just like you did," he said, clearly showing Timothy that his plan to divert him had failed. Timothy laughed aloud though his face remained stern, as if to childishly match Gerald, before rising from his chair abruptly. The sitting three were ready for whatever might come next, their faces stern and muscles tensed. "There you go, Gerald, you and your big mouth!" he shouted as he was just about to strike him with an open palm. But Gerald didn't so much as flinch as his trusty brute was to firmly deal with Timothy's foolish mistake: Abijah arose with unnatural pace and caught the rogue's hand, twisting it into distortion until the assailant's head was on the table. The impact on Timothy's face was so great that a tremendous crunch sounded and all onlookers flinched, even Gerald and Piper, who were no strangers to the horseman's brutal attacks. Timothy's posse, despite clearly being armed in belt and buckle, could not move out of the shock and simply stared as their boss slowly arose from his embarrassment. Slow as it was, there would be no silence to suit. "Fuck" and "Bastard" were amongst the flurry of cusses that were subconsciously spouted during his rising, accompanied with the horrendous view of a crushed nose with copious bleeding.

"Now that should've been done a long time ago," Piper said cockily.

It was only then that one of Timothy's frozen posse acted, pointing a pistol to Piper's face whilst telling him to shut his mouth. This prompted Abijah and Gerald to do the same and, inevitably, the remaining posse followed. Gerald's audacious pistol, flaunting a silver-turquoise design glimmered in the faded light, ready to kill, inscribed with *Silver Death*, the beautiful bullets within saved for a special foe, although he had no hesitation in using one or two of them early.

"No, stop!" Timothy said, his bloody face turned upwards. "Let them perish by him, leave them." His posse lowered their arms and with that, so did the opposing trio. Timothy then instructed his guys with hand gestures to scarper out the pub, which they did albeit slowly whilst maintaining eyes on Gerald and his crew. Timothy was the last to leave but not before gazing at Gerald for a number of uninterrupted seconds, no words said, for his action to leave said enough. Timothy would vacate and Gerald would know Timothy's intentions, or rather lack of. He intended to do nothing, to leave him to hunt Long John. A move of cowardice, those of uneducated mind claimed, but Gerald could see the logic in Timothy's actions. If

Timothy's guys were to shoot Gerald dead and word got out, then his death would be avenged and a bloodbath would occur. But if Long John were to slay him, then his old rival would be dead with no repercussions for Timothy. The three were all who remained in the pub and silence fell for the first few seconds. Gerald gathering his thoughts on what had just happened. But soon enough he broke from his trance, gulped down the remainder of his pint and smashed it against the ground. "Come on then, lads, let's find that damn hotel," he said as he led the way out, Piper and Abijah following close behind.

Throughout the night, the storm persisted in ravaging the borough with high winds and prolific rain. It battered the windows as Gerald looked out onto the empty streets beyond, standing within the walls of the hotel after finally finding it. It was a hotel by name only and was actually just a house that had been rented to them by an old bookkeeper, and as a result, books and bookshelves occupied much of the space though with pleasing effect. One could get lost in the knowledge available here. As Piper and Abijah succumbed to slumber in the other room, Gerald stood at the window whilst the log fire to his left dried him, his mind was fixated on the blackness beyond, just knowing that this fiend was lurking somewhere out there. His hand patted

Silver Death in his belt, knowing one of the bullets within was destined for Long John's head.

Eventually, Gerald broke from his fascination beyond the glass and ventured into the labyrinth of bookshelves behind him. He casually scoured those shelves and though there were many in number, it didn't take him long to find a book that caught the eye. A most relevant piece entitled *The Greats*. A compilation of authors, depicting all Greats up to the present day. Not a more relevant book in the entire labyrinth, Gerald knew. He pulled it from the pile and sat on one of the couches in the corner of the room. His eyes did not blink as they were sickened to see the hideous conjuring of nature, men of abnormal proportion and power, scattered throughout the world. "Greek Greats," "French Greats," "British Greats," "Irish Greats," they have been everywhere. Beside each horrific depiction were the fables attributed to their demise; tales of strong and fearless men who besieged such beasts with fantastical ends. Gerald dared to believe a page could be reserved for him, "I'll kill you, I swear," he whispered to himself. Quiet as it was, it wasn't silent enough to avoid the ears of an individual unknown to him.

"Kill who?" asked the old bookkeeper. Gerald was taken by surprise and turns to his left, not knowing he had entered the room. Gerald wasn't to answer but the bookkeeper's sharp eye ensured he didn't need to, the title of the book saying it all.

"You are here for Long John?" asked the bookkeeper.

"I am," Gerald answered.

The bookkeeper shook his head and began to turn away, "Go home, you fool," he said in the process.

Intolerant to the words, Gerald put the book to one side and stood up abruptly. "I am no fool... I will kill him."

"Many from different paths have tried, but all leave via the same exit. A body bag to the morgue," said the bookkeeper. "He is unkillable."

Gerald reached for the book just behind him and waved it. "These were the same as him, they all met their ends. Killed and buried. I will do the same to him."

The old bookkeeper laughed silently to himself, though loud enough to be heard. "If you think he is like them, you are already dead," he said before exiting the room.

"I will kill him, I will!" Gerald stressed once more. The old bookkeeper took a few steps before stopping to voice once more: "Why now? You know how long he's been here, so why now?"

A solid question, the most solid that could be asked and one that Gerald found to be easily answerable. But was it an answer the old man would be willing to understand? Gerald thought to himself. He hesitated, and consequently, the bookkeeper made his own assumption and answered for him.

"Of course... the money," he said as he went to leave the room, but such an answer prompted Gerald into admission, with now, no regard for how the answer would be perceived.

"It's a small world I live in," he said, which led the old man to stop and listen. "The clans, syndicates, mobs, families or whatever you call them, we know each other, or of each other. And, in this game, perception and reputation is everything. Such a sum attracts the serious lot and with it, all our reputations are at stake. They will be made or broken and whoever comes out on top... he will be a God amongst men. Gold amongst dirt. I will have my place in that book, you mark my words old timer."

The old man was sharp and immediately armed with a response. "I have marked many such words and I'll tell you; you'll never lay waste to that fiend. He's not what's in those pages, they are fabled whereas he is real. A devil of flesh, a beast with senses. We've all seen it and heard of his tragic ways, you won't be any different than the rest who've come."

Gerald felt the subtlest of tremors in his fingertips, the fables now corrupting rather than comforting, and with the bookkeeper appearing to be undeterred, there was only one thing left to say. "I guess we'll have to wait and see who's right," Gerald said as the old man continued to leave the room.

"I am right" he replied. "I always am in the end."

Gerald hears the faint words as the door closes behind him. Alone once more, Gerald retired to the couch but could not relax. His hands still shaking, he muttered the words, "Shut up!" to himself many a time as he tried to shift the doubts away. Fruitless it would be, the doubts lasting long into that endless night.

The morning arrived as the night hours finally ceased. Piper, with Abijah, standing at the doorway, nudged his boss sternly on the arm as Gerald laid asleep on the one-person couch. A baker's dozen eventually did it, Gerald sleeping too deeply to even respond to the first few prods, the most recent nudges gaining a response at last.

"Did you not sleep well, boss?" asked Piper as he and Gerald sat on opposing couches in the book-filled room. Gerald rubbed his eyes and tried to get himself into a position that at least resembled comfort before answering.

"No, not really. Listen, I've been thinking, we may need to send word for additional men to join us from the north."

The response took Piper and Abijah by surprise, with the latter displaying an abrupt facial expression that only Piper saw. It was soon clear to Piper that, given his boss' apparent uneasy night, that an answer would need to be given for this sudden suggestion.

"Can I ask why?" Piper queried. A question that hardly took Gerald by surprise but sparked the strong doubts he felt last night. Nonetheless, an answer would clearly be needed, but in the end just a mindless mumble of unexplained words sounded.

"We just do," he said.

Piper had known Gerald for too long to be fooled and easily recognised his boss' rare moment of doubt. Overthinking, Piper would put it down to. Natural and somewhat foreseen, Piper was quick to act. He arose from his seat and approached his boss, saying, "Boss, you don't need anyone else, you don't even need me or Abijah. What you need is to remember why you are here. Think back to what you said in the carriage. Think of how Abijah wanted to slay that fiend and the words that you said, 'It must be me, no one else.'"

"For I am the face of this family and I must be the one that is fabled," Gerald finished.

Remembering that moment Gerald's back straightened once more and his eyes levelled with Piper's. All the whilst, Abijah was stood at the doorway trying his upmost to bite his tongue. He feared for his boss, a bloodless brother, and feared of the outcome that was more likely than not. This dream of Gerald's, to be the king of his rivals, could see him buried in his own bones. He knew that should half the stories of Long John's terror be true, then Gerald wouldn't stand a chance. Truth was, Gerald did need him here despite Piper's false assurances. Him more than anyone else for it was Abijah alone who was powerful enough to slay the beast, being the only horseman. He wouldn't dare voice it, but should it come to it, he intended to take his boss' role in the slaying should Gerald not be up to demand. An act that saw Abijah immortalised instead and consequently shunned by his brothers, he knew, but necessary should it be the choice between life and death for his boss and friend.

As the trio were stationed in the room of books, Piper who was standing before Gerald noticed something to his left where the window was. The window looked out onto the streets of the markets and the turning of Piper's head revealed a gathering of people in the distance. Down a moderately narrow alley to the right, all eyes were gazing at something. Something beyond the view of the window.

"Everything all right?" asked Abijah as he noticed Piper's initially curious gaze turn into more of a concerned one.

Gerald then also noticed his staring.

"I'm... not sure," Piper said as his eyes shadowed a pair of young women who were curiously pushing their way through the fairly dense crowd to view the subject of its attention. Those women then covered their mouths and screamed horrendously with only a second's gaze at the cause. Piper instinctively ran out the room and headed for the street, with Gerald and Abijah immediately following.

With great haste the three crossed the street and raced to the market, opposite, soon wrestling the gatherers. Their minds conjured up dubious imagery faster than their hearts would pulsate, creating all manners of horrendous scenes, in preparation.

"Could it be him?" Gerald inevitably wondered, his hand holding onto the concealed Silver Death tighter with every approaching step. "Could this be it?" his mind teased. "The moment for my history to be made?" His entire body trembled at the prospect which was soon visible to Abijah, who was running closely behind.

"The stark reality is hitting him," Abijah said to himself, the view ahead of him affirming his doubts in Gerald. He could never give words of false hope, as Piper had innocently done, but could affirm by a far less personal action. Abijah stretched his arm ahead and place his hand on Gerald's shoulder, this being enough for his leader to gain a degree of composure as the shakes suddenly ceased.

The struggling through the crowds became more diificult as the distance between them and the turning of the corner tightened, barely inches between persons.

"Come on, move it!" Piper would demand as he was ahead of the others and barged those who would not listen, his actions making space for Gerald and Abijah to follow more easily. Sudden breezes of air gave a hint to what awaited them, Gerald compelled to choke in the moment. Something that was rotting greatly.

"What in the name of God is that smell?" Abijah asked aloud, but was met with no answer. The turning to the right could never be closer and the trio thought they couldn't go any faster, that was, until a new set of onlookers just ahead saw view of the corner's secret and screamed with ghastly shock. Gerald and the others may as well have averted gravity with the swift movements that followed, and came too to view what the turning possessed.

The three of them no strangers to sickening sights, but this would render them novices. Piper hardly able to hold his breakfast, staunchly stared away with impulse whilst Gerald and Abijah felt drawn to the view. The majority of those viewing, remaining silent as if accustomed to such sights. Whilst Gerald, his posse and those not so toughened would emit a flurry of shocking sounds. It was shocking how some could grow used to

34

this and perhaps more so the fact that such sights existed.

Gerald's eyes dared to sway as a particular onlooker in the crowd stole his attention, only adding to gruesomeness of the borough's custom. A young chap, no older than ten, no more sickened than the majority who stood so stiffly with expressionless faces. Gerald's eyes then returned to the monstrosity, gazing upon the gruesome arrangement of bones, skin and muscles. Shaped as if mocking the shape of man, it was poised against the end wall with fingers used as nails. The multiple heads and limbs, moulded and merged together, would tell this was more than the parts of a single soul. This would be a few men, men whose identities would be known as Gerald noticed the tribal markings across the torn skins. Oh, how the shaking returned and with it the plaguing doubts. Gerald joined Piper in facing the other way, leaving Abijah alone in staring at the devilish conjuring.

"This is no Buddha Patel," Abijah uttered, just loudly enough for his boss to hear, reciting a fact that all but those Bloody Sons knew.

"No, it is not," Gerald silently replied, whilst looking in the opposite direction and sounding as if he was about to vomit.

Abijah hardly blinked for he wanted the view of the hanging Hispanics cemented in his mind, the sternest reminder of what likely awaited his boss should Gerald's crusade persist. Abijah's secret plan then grew bolder, seeing the likelihood of him replacing his boss' role increasing tenfold.

"Good luck," Abijah heard an onlooker mutter sarcastically as he walked past him and Gerald, clearly accustomed to recognising hopefuls here for Long John. Gerald heard this stranger's disrespect but acted as if he hadn't, not so much as meeting eyes with him, too focussed on battling the inner doubts. But the words to follow ensured they couldn't be ignored.

"Long live the long man," said an old lady hidden deep within the crowd, "May all the hoodlums be stricken this way." Words said with no contest, clearly resembling the thoughts of the majority.

The day passed and the sky grew dark, the markets lying almost entirely empty save one person — Gerald, standing lonesome before the decaying corpses, the smell evermore rancid. He had remained there since morning, staying ever still as one soul after another left to resume their day. Eventually he and his posse were all that remained in that rotting alley corner, but even Piper and Abijah were to eventually leave. This was by his request, he wanted to be alone. He needed to think, to comprehend.

To put a person to this sight was terrifying and a cascade of beasts flooded his mind as a result, each more provoking than the last. He stood there alone for quite some time, barely blinking as he made the sight firm in his mind. But finally, he had seen enough, and turned to head for the hotel, nearby. He had turned with purpose, and the immediate view rendered him ready for action.

Instinctively, Gerald gripped the Silver Death beside his buckle with relentless intent, watching the silent figure standing ominously at a distance. But once those eyes of his gained knowledge of what awaited, his tension eased and the grip loosened. A savage trembling, that grew with every second his eyes laid upon the opposing figure. Gerald felt cold and shivered, his breathing beyond his control. This was a sensation far harsher than all such manners before and suddenly Piper's words felt nothing more than a romanticised teasing. He did need Piper and Abijah. Anybody and everybody. Piper's assuring words fell silent in his mind, along with any assurances of his own that he had long prepared for this prophesised moment. There was nothing, his brain being no more useful to him than his Silver Death. The utter inability to use either, ominously shattered by the sight ahead.

The light wind was all that separated them as the fabled fiend, heavily-hunched and with cane, began a stiff approach. Gerald's erratic breathing quickened as he franticly stepped back, looking behind him and seeing only the wall and the freshest victims staring back. Gerald could do nothing other than freeze completely by this point, not even brave enough to step back an inch further. The streets of the market eerily silent, peaceful and deceiving to the dramatic scene unfolding in one of its alleys.

Gerald did nothing and remained perfectly still, knowing that this could only be one person, his heart pulsing never harder, and every limb trembling though he tried his dandiest not to show it. The tall fiend took large steps as he approached Gerald, the sheer height of it enabling the widest strides. The figure would then lean down to Gerald, until their faces met. Any hint of control in Gerald's composure, now entirely absent.

His face, that terrible face, the very one that so many horrific tales were ascribed to, now just inches away. The hour of night serving as a blessing in not unveiling the whole horror, though the moon in a near cloudless sky begrudgingly ensured enough could be known. The face was desperately warped as if it had turned anti-clockwise and stopped midway, and the eyes heavily squinted in paving the way for the exaggerated smile which dominated and stretched up and across much of it. A horrid sight, on a par with the one its hands had conjured just behind Gerald, the display's rotting smell no longer the greatest offence to the senses. The fiend's typical Victorian attire was all that resembled normality and even luxury, clean and straight. The suit, brown and continuous in all elements from top to bottom. High-waisted trousers and long coat, all the same shade. The top hat to cap it all, itself brown and also of fine make, though the thin grey hair extending downwards did nothing to complement it. The sheer arch in his back, testimony to his colossal height, easily twelve feet if stood fully upright. His legs hideously long and thin to allow such a standing, but the other limbs were no less abnormal. The arms, neck, pelvis, all churningly-distorted and stretched with not a hint of normality present.

As Long John's glare invading Gerald's space, he was trapped and could do nothing other than stare straight into those eyes. The breath and the smell, leaving nothing to the imagination, also couldn't be avoided — rancid and stomach-churning. But those eyes were the worst, for they were windows to the soul. The simple and most instinctive way of knowing a person, unveiling their intentions and motives. In Gerald's way of life, he had grown accustomed to knowing the eyes of men, but it couldn't be said of the abomination before him. Those windows were shuttered and soulless, not an ounce of humanity within them. No motive, no man, just a monster. Hell knows if he can grasp why he is, eternal damnation for any who can tell him why. Living to take the living, a demon, if ever such a thing existed.

The Mayor, the bookkeeper, the stories. Gerald knew how right they all were.

Long John then stood back up as far as his crooked spine would allow and gaze upon that hideous creation he had made, just the night before, like an old master observing his own art. It was only then that Gerald felt the blessing of breathing fully again and started so with sharp intakes. He'd felt as if he was about to die, but of course, that moment could still be coming. He looked up at him as Long John stared at the rotting corpses with an inanimate face, not a single part of it twitching nor tweaking. The monstrous murderer passed Gerald with those lengthy strides to gaze upon the Hispanics more closely, and, whether of bravery or idiocy, Gerald took the chance.

With little conscious thought, he reached Silver Death, grasping for it as gently and smoothly as he was able.

"Come on, just do it." He inwardly trembled as he raised the weapon sharply. But that sudden movement led the fiend to abruptly turn, his eyes locking back onto Gerald immediately, but Gerald's hand did nothing but tremble.

"Come on... come on you coward," Gerald said, this time aloud, as the moment presented itself. But though his finger hovered around the trigger, it was frozen in pressing. If anything, the hand shook more than ever as advancing, those longest of legs teased Gerald's inferiority.

He retraced his strides back to him, arching down to gaze Gerald, dead in the eye once again, with Gerald's pounding heart acting as loud as that absent bullet should have been. But Silver Death wasn't to know smoke as it should and stayed cold, Gerald's fear consuming him so entirely, he even lowered his arm. His face hosted a degree of displays in that moment, all united in showing fear. The facial muscles hurting, never being exposed to such actions, all whilst Long John's remained still. The fiend stared long enough to leave Gerald's inferiority just short of soiling itself before granting the blessing of its departure.

The fable then rose to his full height once more, and passed him, heading away with those abnormal strides.

Gerald was left frozen, as he tried to grapple with the encounter in his mind. There had been no words, none to be said nor thought. Nothing could have prepared him for that, for the rarest feeling, something he was a stranger to. That not of fear but of something far deeper, yet fear would be the only word known for it. A true injustice, for it could never be told of, but it could be shared — shared with the souls of those who had encountered such a beast in this way and lived to tell their tales. Gerald was ashamed and embarrassed for how he felt, like a young boy screaming from a nightmare, but what was to follow saw it replaced with something else. What followed would be natural for a proud man like him, natural but far from smart.

A tremor echoed throughout and across all avenues of the market, with an aftermath that would surely spell Gerald's end. The shell nervously landed beside a bewildered man who just watched as the bullet bounced off Long John's arched back, the fiend not to even so much as looking back and acknowledging him.

"No fables, only facts," Gerald said to himself as he watched the fiend fade into the night. Like a wolf to a den, a wolf beyond the effects of bullets. The scared little boy who feared the dark, left alone in the alley. Piper's words of wisdom, now known as all-out lies.

The sun was seen once more and thus a night of hideous revelation came to an end. Gerald barely slept and was making a conscious effort to contain his insecurities. He looked half dead after spending most of the night at the side of his bed, swaying back and forth as if mindless. Many times, he relived the events of the night, teasing what could've been done differently, but he could find no plausible solution. Every outcome was the same; Long John walking away triumphant. Gerald knew the triumphant walk to be nothing more than a tease, knowing in reality the fiend would again walk away with no care in the world — just as it had last night.

As the sun was still in its amber infancy, Gerald got to his feet and dragged himself beyond his room, down the stairs to the book room. He grasped the only book of interest and inflamed his mind with the illustrations of The Greats and with reading of their epic downfalls. Tears were held back in that moment, with tremendous effort.

He then began to hear footsteps descending the stairs behind the wall, Gerald composed his posture and acted as if all was fine. He was expecting to see the bookkeeper, but surprised to see his horseman emerge instead. Abijah walked in the room and sat on the seat opposite.

"Is everything all right, boss?" he asked.

Gerald knew just how futile his efforts of secrecy were, his horseman knowing him too well. To respond with words in vain would serve no purpose, Gerald knew, and so the waters of shame were to flow.

The face his boss presented was one unlike any Abijah had seen and he knew one behemoth of a revelation was coming, and with it, a sole cause came to mind.

"I was wrong," Gerald simply said, the words of doubt confirming what Abijah had guessed.

"Long John," Abijah shouted internally. How foolish he considered himself for heeding his boss' order and leaving him alone in the market long into the night, Abijah guessing that's when this encounter occurred. "Long John," Abijah abruptly responded, not in question but affirmation, to which Gerald hauntingly nodded.

Gerald continued, "I was wrong… to think that I could be the one to kill him."

Abijah said nothing in response and just sat there with the sincerest of stares. If he were Piper, he would stop his boss short and interject with false assurances that Gerald could do it, but Abijah was no liar. To Abijah, what Gerald was claiming wasn't a revelation to him but rather the simple affirmation of what he already knew. "It must be you" Gerald then said with the tightest of tongues, knowing that only a horseman could cease this beast. Abijah didn't protest or rejoice in the matter, but instead quietly took solace in knowing that his intended actions would now be blessed by his boss.

"What was he like?" Abijah soon asked, knowing of the encounter without being told.

Gerald seemed reluctant to speak of it but eventually his voice came, knowing that not talking of the beast only added to the fable. "Tall, as they say." Gerald tried to speak with relaxed composure, "With a cane and crooked back, joints of unnatural disposition. I shot him… right in his back and…"

Abijah encouraged him with a hand gesture but told himself to be more patient as the face of his boss grew visibly more distressed — as if he was holding a roar of anguish within. Abijah's knowledge that Gerald was besieged by emotions was correct, and he had to compose his voice before uttering another word. What he was to say next would tell it all; his failure and the beast's triumph. The next sentence no more than a word, the hardest to ever say. And, even despite much effort of restraint, Gerald's admission was still loud and tearful. "Nothing!" he roared, "It did nothing!" Gerald wiped those tears, leaving Abijah to lower his head in respect to his boss and reverence to Long John. The fight awaiting him, now fully ordained.

Later that day, with Piper too arisen, the trio roamed the streets of that sizeable market, crowded with souls and sales. Those walls of the hotel were to plague Gerald's mind, reminding him of his failure the previous night, and so he avoided them for his own sanity. Gerald had begun the walk with a sorrow stance, drooping with a dull face, but found the vibrancy of the market infectious and thus that hideous night was pushed further to the back of his mind. He was far from happy, perhaps the most miserable ever, but had unexpectedly found solace in the buzzing atmosphere.

It known to the three of them that, contrary to how the night portrayed it, the Sparks borough was indeed a vibrant place with buzzing markets and people — just like the rest of London. One could even dare to forget the beast that roamed God knows how near, but then again, these souls didn't know any better and were evidently familiar with living with a monstrosity lurking about. That fiend could be anywhere, possibly around any of the market corners, but nobody raised an eyebrow to it. Pitiful, or brave? Either way, Gerald and his posse took delight in such a revelation and were even tempted to indulge in the beverages on offer. "Boss, this place... it's..." Piper said. "...Amazing" Abijah would finish. "It is... but stay focussed," their boss told them, ensuring they were still aware of the threat that could show its distasteful face behind any corner.

The brazen smell of bread and cakes spread throughout the market and Gerald noticed it very quickly, a smell of childhood and simpler times. They all noticed and commented of its tremendous smell. "Wow," Abijah simply said, no further words needed. Piper may as well have started drooling like a mutt to a bone by this point. Tempting as it was for them to go inside the nearby bakery, they were not to forget Gerald's earlier words and intended to pass through with much reluctance. That is, until the appearance of a man made it more difficult than it already was.

A sweaty man in a baker's apron emerged from the bakery and invited them to come in, as if fate would have it no other way. "Please gentlemen, come in and taste the finest bread that Sparks has to offer," he said in what sounded like a business slogan. The three looked at one another and though Gerald was reluctant at first, not wanting to go against his own words, he eventually yielded and accepted the baker's invitation. Though, not completely relaxing his worries, Gerald instructed Abijah to remain outside and keep an eye out for any trouble — promising to bring out a bun for him. His horseman did as instructed, and awaited on a thrice-legged stool at the corner of the bakery, watching cautiously for any unsavoriness ahead as the others followed the baker inside.

The bakery had no customers and yet the smell was ever inviting as the baker pulled out their seats and invited them to get themselves comfortable before presenting them with a host of bread and cakes. It was heavenly and certainly revived nostalgic memories, every bite inviting nothing but bliss.

"You like it?" the baker asked rather nervously and with stiff frame.

"Oh, incredible," Piper answered with his mouth full of food.

Gerald glanced up at the baker, noticing the unusual sweating and tense pose, and placed the slice of cake in his hand back on the table. Unsure whether to be concerned, Gerald queried the perceived kindness before taking a further bite.

"Tell me, why are you doing this?" he asked politely though with stern cheeks.

"Well, you see… it's… well it's… it's a new line of product and I needed… someone to try them," the baker finally answered.

"And that's why you're sweating like that?" Gerald queried, Piper ceasing in his feast to stare at the baker by this point.

"Yes, yes exactly… very nervous about it, sir. Very nervous," the baker answered, as if helped in the moment.

The baker and Gerald stared at one another for a moment with only silence separating them, and what made for a tense moment was soon to be broken by Piper's interruption.

"Well, I got to tell you, there's nothing to worry about," he said as he scoffed once more, "These… are amazing!"

The baker sighed in presumed relief and headed for the counter, with Gerald yet to resume eating, yet to be fully convinced.

Minutes passed, more and more, one after the other. Abijah, sitting outside up the street, grew bored and sighed for the waiting became tedious. He looked behind and through the window at Piper eating away like a piglet. Abijah smiled to himself in that moment, Piper always falling to food. But then, a view greeted him upon turning back that would ensure that the smile quickly faded. He squinted before arising to his feet, needing to affirm what his eyes were showing him. That group, standing out amongst the masses, what were those cowboys up to?

Seeing them was cause for concern on its own, for of course these were their hunting grounds too, but how they were acting caused even more alarm. Charles Black and his posse were crouched and moving with purpose nearby.

"What the…?" Abijah said aloud to himself as he stood on the stool in the hopes of granting a greater view. Nothing significant was gained by it, as the cowboys were still hardly in view. They soon advanced into an alley entirely beyond Abijah's view as he returned to the ground. Something didn't seem right, Abijah knew — those cowboys moving the way they did. Discreet and furtively, as if in pursuit of something. Abijah couldn't be certain but was familiar enough with the actions of a squad on a run-up, but there was only one way to know for sure.

He looked back through the baker's window, ready to knock and shout, but his hand hesitated against the glass. Why say anything, he wondered, what would be the point of it? Gerald had granted Abijah permission to end the beast and so, Abijah was left thinking as to what purpose it would serve for the others to be there. "No," Abijah said to himself, "You'll only put them at risk." Abijah then discreetly moved away from the baker's window, not wanting the others inside to notice any sudden movements, and merged with the crowds just ahead. With a heavy heart he dared look back — Gerald and Piper were blissfully unaware, and Abijah would know the sensation of trembling, for the first time as the alley down which the cowboys had vanished grew ever closer. It took him by surprise as he stared down at his wavering hands, twitching in all directions. "Just nerves," he would tell himself, adopting a certain friend's method of assurance.

"Boss, what's wrong? Lost your appetite all of a sudden?" Piper asked, crumbs splurging everywhere. Gerald wouldn't answer with any degree of haste and instead keep eyes on the baker, now standing at the back of the room. He was facing the back wall, in a pitiful attempt to act normal. Had Gerald been a simple man, he would've assumed the old baker was paying close attention to the menu in front of him. But Gerald could guess the baker's eyes drifted to the clock above.

"No, I'm fine," Gerald replied, just loud enough for Piper's ears, "Just... thinking is all."

"Thinking?" Piper responded, "About what?"

Gerald wouldn't answer and maintain focus on the baker, more so now as the old man began to stroll to his right. Piper finally broke from his feasting and see his boss staring in the direction away from him. Piper follow his gaze and saw the old man behind him. They watched as the baker subtly walked to the right, as though it was no coincidence that a door laid in that direction. The baker's eyes remained firmly in the opposite direction from his two customers, maintaining this foolish act of discretion, before suddenly scarpering through the door once it was within inches.

At once, the pair leapt from their seats, their chairs flying as they reached for their guns. But the swift action proved not swift enough as a man with a gun jumped into the room via the door the baker had scarpered through, followed by the emergence of two other man entering via the bakery's front, also pointing guns. They were surrounded by unforeseen assailants, unforeseen but not unknown for long.

"What do you think you're doing?" Piper demanded.

The triplets snorted and laughed before Gerald added, "We're not the target here!"

The brothers' laughter then subsided and was immediately replaced by an aggressive outburst from one of the brothers, James. "Shut your fucking mouths!" he shouted as his grip tightened around his gun.

Not having any other choice, Gerald and Piper would comply with the demand and were silent. The pair were greatly confused, an emotion apparent in the discreet looks they gave one another. "Where is supposed ceasefire?" Gerald thought to himself, "Why are they doing this?" But the pair were to have their answer, though it would do nothing to change the situation they found themselves in.

Jakub, the more well-spoken of the three explained:

"Initially, no, but after seeing what happened to those foolish Mexicans, we realised that we didn't want to end up as flesh and bones besieged by flies. And so, we had an epiphany so to speak and have spoken with a lovely lady by the name of Chiara De Sorbo. We trust you know the name?"

Gerald shook his head the second that woman's name was uttered, for he knew exactly where the conversation was heading. This woman, head of the whore houses in the eastern boroughs, had had an altercation with the Coffin Bearers only a couple of years back. A fateful action by one of Gerald's own men that led to the brutal killing of her husband.

"Guido's wife," Gerald said.

"Yes, exactly," Jakub replied.

"She's offered a very generous sum for your head. Of course, it's not as valuable as Long John's but it will do," Jensen finished.

"Get on your fucking knees!" the aggressive James then demanded as the brothers clicked their pistols. An inescapable fate quickly approaching, Gerald discreetly turned to the bakery's window on the right. But Abijah's stool was empty. His eyes widened with despair, knowing his horseman wasn't there. He looked to Piper with the gloomiest of gazes. Piper looked back with a glance that needed no words. "Where was he?" With his horseman missing, Gerald knew there was only one card to play in such a scenario, though it was humiliating. But he saw no choice and considered himself damned and humiliated should the Turner Triplets of all people be his end. He would bargain, for the first time since his adolescent days.

"How much is she paying you?" he asked them.

"More than you're worth, now get on your knees!" answered Jensen as the other brothers laughed.

"I'm serious, how much?" asked Gerald, still standing.

"Get on your fucking knees!" shouted James as he pointed the gun straight at him, the muzzle just inches away.

Piper got to his knees at this point, leaving his boss to stand and spear the plea.

Jakub halted his brother for a moment: "Now, hang on a minute James. It's twenty-five thousand if you must know," he answered.

53

"I'll give you thirty — to walk away right now," proposed Gerald.

Piper looked at him with shock and the triplets with surprise. As Gerald had foreseen, there was hesitation within the eyes of the trio and he saw a host of thoughts scale their minds, eventually culminating in a response that at least hinted at consideration.

"We'll have to see it first," Jensen replied.

"Yeah, come on, let's see it!" shouted James.

The proposition had been gifted and received, Gerald knew, but the hardest part was yet to come. The part where all he could do was promise.

"You'll get it as soon as I take the bounty for Long John, I swear," said Gerald with the highest sincerity.

The triplets laughed in near hysterics and couldn't believe his bullish attempt to plea. "You're full of falsehoods, Gerald, always have been! Now for the last time, on your knees!" said an insulted Jakub.

Out of options and nowhere to go, Gerald joined Piper in bending his knees and heading for the ground. "This was it." His brain teased in a fashion reminiscent of the night before, his body shook and his chest tightened.

James stood before the pair of them as Gerald's knees hit the ground. Fate seemed to be pointing to the fact that it was over for them both, a notion reflected in their eyes as they gazed at each other, and as the James' finger tensed over the trigger. Fate is cruel, but not always for what it tells, but rather what it teases, and fate was to hand them one foul joke, for what came next was up to them.

With no hint, an abrupt outburst of gunfire was heard, and screaming commenced as a host of panicked passers stampeded throughout the market. Such a change in events inevitably led most in the bakery to turn their heads towards the window and witness the commotion, the triplets included, but Gerald and Piper were not to be so careless and certainly were not to pass such an opportune moment, focussing on the bewildered James.

The flurry of souls stampeded the market, running in unison in a particular direction. Unified save one, as Abijah struggled against them in the opposite direction and finally breaking free to dash for the alley corner. The sounds foretold the view to come, far harsher than the shrieks in those fearful screams. Abijah even looked back for a moment to see the backs of the heads of all the market goers. Abijah needed no telling who those cowboys were heading for and soon he was to view it. Turning the alley corner, Long John stood amongst a pool of entrails as he duelled with the last victim.

"Bastard!" Charles Black roared as he struck the beast with such a backhand, it echoed beyond Abijah's ears and overpowered the fading screams of the fleeing masses. But it did nothing, the monstrosity did not so much as flinch, and the cowboy horseman was to learn that his anticlimactic strike was the last he'd ever swing, Long John, crushing his head as if it were glass before discarding the fresh corpse. The beast saw Abijah before Charles had even hit the soil, entirely unfazed by the second horseman's presence. Even now, as Abijah shakenly raises his weapon, the monster was inanimate, as if dead. His eyes expressionless as they pierced into Abijah's, the horseman readying the fateful shot.

James laid on the ground, screaming from host of snapped digits, whilst Gerald rained down punches on Jensen as he was mounted on top. Piper was being tossed across multiple tables and was soon on the floor before Jakub grabbed a severed chair leg and started pressing it against his throat. His boss saw the struggle, and with a glance behind and was quick to view one of the guns that had been shifted in the initial struggle, shadowed beneath an overturned table. Gerald lunged from the battered brother beneath him in pursuit of the weapon but found James catching him mid-flight to hammer him with his only good hand.

"You bastard, Gerald!" the aggressive James shouted, "Look what you did to my damn hand!" James then landed a multitude of blows against Gerald's face before making a dash for the gun himself. Before he could get it and turn to fire, Gerald had risen like a man possessed and was instantly countering him. There was a tremendous tug for the gun, intense enough by itself for the battered Gerald but made even more so by the sharp approach of a semi-conscious Jensen. Time was of the essence and Gerald took advantage of James' single hand, pulling the gun from his grasp and shooting him before the approaching brother. Jakub released Piper's neck upon the revelation and went to bludgeon Gerald with all his might, but not making it halfway before joining his brothers on the bloody floor.

"Where the hell is Abijah?" Piper shouted, choking and gasping heavily.

"A very good question," Gerald replied sternly, angered by his horseman's absence.

Gerald approached Piper and aided him to his feet before walking over to the window of the bakery, where he was alarmed by the complete emptiness of the market — not a soul in sight.

"Whoa, where is everyone?" Piper asked, his cough persisting.

"Scarpered," his boss answered as he gazed firmly on the ominous view beyond.

"Yeah, but where?" asked Piper.

A host of ill thoughts flooded Gerald's mind, all culminating in a single cause as he refrained from a speculative answer.

"Viscous little bastards," Piper said as he looked behind him to see the lifeless bodies. "I mean, I always thought people called them fighters, ironically, but obviously not."

Gerald wouldn't answer and instead left the bakery without warning, opening the door and walking with purpose up the market.

"Abijah!" shouted Gerald with Piper in close pursuit, his voice echoing far across the empty streets. As expected, the sound of nothingness matched the empty view. The pair struggled to comprehend what surrounded them, or lack of it, a total state of nothingness, in London, of all places. A vibrant and buzzing market only moments ago, now a ghost town as if long deserted.

"I wonder what those gunshots were about" Piper said with concern, likely having an idea already.

Gerald didn't respond and instead, continued to call his horseman's name. The pair's worry grew with each step, as they cautiously trekking ever further up the single-way street. Standing on debris left by the mass of fleeing people, his voice echoing in the silence, Gerald shouted, "Abijah, where are you?"

Gerald shouted again, with added dread for his valued friend. His voice cracked, emotions making a rare display with Piper present.

"Boss, he'll be all right. He probably went with the crowd," Piper said, falling back on his false assurances once more. But such words would not trick Gerald this time, seeing no logic in his highly-skilled horseman fleeing like a gazelle. No, with the evacuation of the masses and the gunfire, Gerald saw only one likely scenario. Even imagining the event caused him grief and so he picked up the pace with heightened anxiety.

"Abijah!" he shouted more frequently, Piper soon doing the same out of identical concern.

Neither had said it and yet both knew what the other thought, a thought they hoped would be untrue. They were in tremendous distress, shouting his name profusely, but the turning of the bend would reveal utter devastation and Gerald was crushed to his knees, screaming "No!"

Piper gasped and Gerald began to breathe erratically, "No!" he would chant at the scene ahead, foreseen and yet not so, a sickening display of unwritten sin.

The horsemen were hanging as one from a tangled spine, the others mocking a hanging dock beneath them. Gerald's horseman, brute and friend, now nothing more than refuge for rodents. In silence, one by one, people began to return to the market. There as hardly a sound between them, and Gerald, with his face now painted in the dirt from grief, didn't notice them until light gasps began to sound, the gasps only multiplying with the arrival of more eyes upon the godless creation. Gerald looked up towards Piper with a broken-hearted expression. His friend was deformed, demeaned and deceased. Never to walk by his side again, a reality that saw Gerald scream aloud — those screams echoing far beyond the melodies of men.

As the sun grew mellow above the busy hour to the south of the borough, the conjurer of the bloodbath walked fittingly amongst the inhabitants of mere men, beneath him. All would walk near him, even mothers with their young, making no efforts to avoid him. Despite what he had done, despite what he could do, none viewed him any differently to the many other walkers around. Few would even tilt their heads to view his face or so much as focus on his hideous distortions. The beast would change his pace to compensate for the elderly ahead and even alter his direction for on comers. Normal and natural, as if he were nothing more than a man. Such sights would serve as testimony to the stories ascribed to the people of this place, tales of how they walked fearlessly beside him. It would also prove the truth of Timothy's words of the people's acceptance of the fiend. Accepting him into their daily lives.

When he was calm, there was little to worry about, but when he grew angered, such as by invading assailants so foolishly hired, he became murderous and all in their tight minds fled.

With his mammoth hunch and loud-sounding cane echoing against the ground, he was no secret. Many were to walk within inches of him, though gradually dispersing as Long John transcended a particular street. They were concerned for what was likely to happen, their cause for concern being conjured by those poorly-concealed weapons on a man whose reputation was beyond the realm of discretion. The people would evade with fear and yet Long John walked as if he hadn't seen what awaited him, when in truth, his height enabled him to see long before anyone else had.

Facing him from a distance was a man feared by the boldest, revered in many fable — respected by even his most ghastly of foes. He was viewed by many as the strongest horseman on the planet with a record that was impossible to deny, with uncountable bounties behind him. A single army, standing stern as his latest tally was to rise soon. After a few rapid escapes of those who remained, the street was an empty shell as the two sides of the colossal coin stood in opposition. Five metres apart, Stanley's hands unapologetically wavered around his belt as the fiend remained expressionless.

The strongest of all men hen stiffly approached the stern mammoth, taking slow but sure steps, the thudding of his feet the only echo in that dissolute street. The horseman wouldn't halt until mere inches separated them. Stanley, equipped with a piece of his arsenal pointed it upwards. As he cocked his pistol, the fabled fiend bent down to view his assailant more closely. Long John stared as their faces lay centimetres apart, but he saw no eyes and only a mask.

The two titans simply stared at one another and no tension was visible. The brave or foolish onlookers from either end of the street stared and gossiped, their indecipherable whispers echoing past them. This was a first for them, seeing the beast act in such a way. He leant in even closer, their faces advancing to physical contact, but the horseman wasn't to retreat. Through his infamous mask, Stanley looked straight into the eyes of the fiend and saw the same motionless and distorted smile that many others had seen just before their fates were determined. Those eyes, dismal and dull, showing nothing. There was no fear, no anger, and no resentment. Simply nothing.

After a few seconds, Stanley walked around Long John and advanced up the street beyond, passing gasping onlookers in the process. Long John turned his head and his eyes followed the horseman until he was beyond his overseeing view.

The fiend, gaining only greater renown, continued his aimless travelling with his cane echoing on the ground once more. The event that took place, or rather which didn't, spread like a plague throughout the ears of the witnesses.

The sun rose for another day; the streets and their markets buzzing once more, but beyond the dandy light of day lay a firmly set darkness and depression within the hotel. An atmosphere within that, should the weather replicate it, would devolve the clear skies into a gloomy grey with the harshest hail.

"Boss, what are we going to do now?" asked Piper as the two sit in the book room, with the curtains closed.

"I... I don't know," said a disheartened Gerald. He was at great conflict within himself. He knew logically that he'd have either to retreat or send for more men, but knew that neither were really feasible options. If his horseman, the strongest in his ranks, couldn't besiege the beast, then sending for simple men appeared pointless. And retreating, he thought, would leave his pride forever wounded. And so, with both options toppled, Gerald found himself considering a third option — one he would only council with himself. Insane and suicidal, he knew, but he was considering the option of a final assault — where he would go against the game and charge at the bull. Rather that, than bringing more men to die, and leaving and allowing his rivals to take the trophy. His mind was made up, almost, as his eyes drifted to his Silver Death on the desk beside him. Gerald was close to voicing the third option, even calling for Piper's attention, but found himself interrupted by an abrupt knock at the door.

Paranoid but prepared, Gerald arose from his dented seat and grabbed his Silver Death before drawing the curtains harshly. The bookkeeper had already answered the door by the time those curtains were drawn and the soon-to-be-known knocker was already being granted entry.

"What the fuck?" Gerald said, upon seeing the sight, just seeing the entering figure in time.

"Boss, what is it?" Piper asked, not seeing who it was.

"I don't' fucking believe this, be ready!" Gerald ordered him as he raised his Silver Death to the door of the book room with Piper soon following suit. The bookkeeper entered first, with the person of concern close behind, and Gerald interrupted whatever words of welcome the bookkeeper was to give.

"Hands raised, now!" Gerald demanded at the top of his voice. The bookkeeper would evade the man behind him as the other did as he was told. Those hands went straight up, revealing an empty belt beneath. But Gerald was to take no chances and ordered Piper to search him, whilst Gerald maintained aim. After a quick and stern search, an assuring nod from Piper indicated nothing had been found.

"Right, down on your knees" Gerald said, as Piper pushed the visitor down. This was followed by an order for the bookkeeper to vacate the room, which he did.

"What the hell are you doing here?" Gerald demanded, with the man on his knees and arms to the back of his head. The man who had entered so brazenly was Benjamin, a prominent member of Helmswood and trusted advisor to Abel Rees.

"I'm here by request of Mr Rees," he answered.

"Yeah, no shit! What does he want?" Gerald demanded to know as he pointed his Silver Death into Benjamin's cheek.

"He wanted me to give you this," he said as he reached for his pocket.

"What do you think you're doing?" shouted Gerald as he clicked his Derringer.

"Easy, it's just a letter," he replied.

Benjamin slowly pulled out the letter and Gerald snatched it from his hand.

"What is it?" asked Piper.

Gerald was silent for a minute as he read the letter, whilst still aiming, before smiling in disbelief at its contents.

He gave it to Piper. "Is he joking, does he think I'm a fool?" Gerald asked with an aggressive expression and cocking his gun.

The letter had suggested a truce, along with the request for a meeting with his arch-rival.

"No, not at all," Benjamin insisted.

"You can be armed if you wish, it's just an invite to talk about Long John is all."

Gerald took the letter from Piper and scrunched it before throwing it at Benjamin's face.

"There's nothing to talk about," he said.

"But there is, I can assure you," Benjamin persisted.

"You see, you and Abel have something the other needs. And, with those combined, there may be a way to turn the tide."

"'Turn the tide'? What the hell are you on about?" Piper teased. "Boss, let's just chop him up and send him back." Piper looked to his boss, expecting a unified response, but found a look of consideration in his eyes. "Boss?" Piper asked, but Gerald was still thinking.

He looked Benjamin in the eye, thinking of the words he said.

"What do you mean by turning the tide, and what are these things the other needs?" Gerald queried.

Benjamin lightly shook his head saying, "It's not for me to say. Meet Abel and you'll see."

Gerald unscrewed the mangled paper and saw the address at its bottom, the Carson Garage. With a final look at Benjamin's sincere expression, an answer was to be known.

"Get out," Gerald said.

"Boss?" asked Piper as his head turns to him with a confused expression.

"Get out, go!" Gerald told Benjamin once more, at which he arose and quickly scarpered.

"Boss, surely we're not…?" questioned Piper.

"If there is a path to ending this, then I shall walk it," said Gerald as he stared Piper dead in the eye.

Gerald went to exit the room but stopped at the voice of his ally.

"That 'path' leads to home," Piper said.

Gerald glanced back just before leaving. "I have nothing if I retreat, damn me if I go back now, but should you want to flee then so be it," he said.

Piper was deep in thought for a moment as Gerald remained still. He had concerns, great concerns about trusting their arch enemy, but perhaps he was being naïve and misunderstanding the strategy of his leader. Perhaps he would need to realise that Abel and his goons were no longer the enemy, at least not for now. Like two lions charging at a buffalo separately, it was too dangerous. Only together could they bring the beast tumbling down. Gerald's friend and sole ally uttered no words, only a nod, and for the first time a smile would breach that besieged face.

The sky glowed golden, for the night was steadily approaching. Gerald and Piper were walking the streets of northern Sparks, heading towards the Carson Garage as requested. They were armed as the letter said they may be, not that they did it for that reason, for even if it said otherwise, they were not taking any chances. Abel Rees was Gerald's rival and had been for over a decade. For years the two groups had taken territory, business, trade and men from one another in an endless game of foehood. And despite all that, Gerald found himself walking willingly into a scenario entirely controlled by his adversary. He halted as the garage came into view to hear the words of doubts one last time. Such words were no different than the ones that sounded upon contemplating the letter; that of reconsideration, fear and even retaliation. But the doubts weren't loud enough to shun the voice of belief in this path being worth the risk and so he would persist with no further hesitation.

The Carson Garage was in sight and the pair were just minutes away, but the approach of an unexpected figure caused them to stop in their tracks. He had just emerged from an alley not far to their right. "Is that… who I think it is?" asked Piper.

Gerald hesitated in disbelief. He found it surprising that he saw the soul in this way, walking with his head lowered as if ashamed, with his eyes refusing to accept the sight.

"It is, though it shouldn't be," Gerald answered.

The pair's eyes were firm on the king of horsemen, but Stanley wasn't to acknowledge their approaching presence until he had brushed Gerald's shoulder upon passing. The budging of the shoulder, no matter its lightness, led an emotional Stanley into an outburst and he grabbed Gerald firmly by the shirt before even laying eyes on him to see who he was.

"What the hell do you think you're doing?" said Gerald.

"You should watch where you're going!"

Piper armed himself and pointed the gun at Stanley's head. Stanley was quick to release him, though Gerald was certain the gun to his cranium had nothing to do with it. Gerald could only be so confident, not able to see the horseman's face, but he could sense a fragility within him. He had the sense that Stanley had dropped him because he simply had no desire to fight. Defeated and deflated, Gerald would guess — a theory that was soon proved to be correct.

"Leave, you won't defeat him," the horseman said in a tone that was withered and weak. "I looked into those eyes, utterly lifeless. A beast like that will not fall I tell you." Stanley then barged past the pair with no further words, hastily retreating beyond the clear view of their eyes.

Gerald and Piper donned the most bewildered of looks, the words being far from anything they could've expected just two days ago.

"What the hell happened to him?" Piper asked aloud.

Gerald's eye turned to the retreating horseman, not breaking sight until he was beyond a spec, whilst Piper's question playing over in his mind. A good question, one that Stanley would certainly never answer, although Gerald doubted an answer would be needed.

Piper wouldn't understand the ordeal but Gerald could and prayed his ally never would experience it. The feeling one feels when the piercing gaze of Long John strips a man battered and bruised. Leaves the proudest utterly powerless, a feeling of pure inadequacy and inferiority. Leaving only a shell of their past selves intact, the rest being ripped out of them without a hand being raised. That would be his most devastating aspect, the part that isn't spoken of. Not damage to the body, but instead within.

"Something terrible," Gerald was finally able to say, holding back much emotion himself.

"Nothing but a coward!" Piper harshly added.

"No, he is the bravest of us all" Gerald said to himself, admiring the horseman's will to retreat.

The golden sky was no longer existent by the time Gerald and Piper made it to the garage. With their approach, the pair noticed two of Abel's men standing at the entrance. Eli and Nathan. To the untrained eye, they seemed unarmed, but Gerald could see the slight bulges to the left side of their coats. It was too late to reconsider now. Gerald patted his Silver Death, making it obvious he was ready for a fight, should Abel go south on his proposal, and the men opened the garage door without eye contact. Gerald and Piper did the same as they entered, the volatile history between them being easily provoked. The door was closed behind them.

Inside the garage were only Abel, Benjamin and Jude, guns concealed but visibly prepared. Abel sat on one end of the table, the only feature in the dissolute space, with his trusted boys to either side. Gerald advanced to the table that stood at the space's centre, holding onto his concealed Silver Death with Piper following respectfully behind. Gerald wasn't to level his gaze with his rival until his backside hit the chair opposite, allowing himself to compose himself in the presence of a man who he hated equally to the fiend. Even with his seating, there would be a number of seconds before the two gazed upon the other, hatred in clear view to even a blind man. The bloodbath pursued by the two of them, too much to forgive, and yet here they both were. Neither happy enough to voice it, but clearly both accepting that something meaningful could stem from this gathering.

"Well, I'm waiting Abel" said Gerald as he soon grew inpatient.

"You know why we are here, yes?" Abel asked sternly.

"Not really, no," Gerald sighed, "Your boy Benjamin says we've got something the other needs and frankly, I'm dead confused as to what the fuck that means."

Abel shook his head over the frank response, clearly not accustomed to being spoken to in this way, his fists trying not to clench in a physical display of provocation. "I'll get to the point then" Abel then said with restraint.

"Yes, please do," Gerald sharply followed.

After a brief pause, inhaling as if readying for protest, Abel continued, "The Mexicans and the Yanks are dead, it's obvious that we are just going to get picked off one at a time if we go at him alone. What we need is a coordinated attack with a collective plan."

"Right?" said Gerald, waiting for the bombshell he sensed coming.

"It's abundantly clear that this bastard cannot be killed with simple bullets or weapons. Bullets just spray off him like rain," Abel continued. "And so I got thinking, what if we need to strike in a specific place with perfect precision. Like killing a grizzly or boar, striking them in just the right place will send them tumbling down."

"Just, get to the point" hurried Gerald, unimpressed with Abel words of comparing this beast to simple animals.

Abel then gestured to Benjamin, on his left, as if signalling for something. Gerald grew nervous, ready for one of Abel's antics — Piper too who was standing behind. But what was to follow was the emergence of an item: A tool of some kind, very thin with the sharpest point. Silver-coated, as if a knife but only sharper and thinner. "Leon Lachlan conjured this titan killer for me," Abel explained as he was handed the strange item. "Tailored perfectly and in such little time. 'Brain Stake' I call it."

"The Brain Stake?" Piper laughed uncontrollably, but with a dead reception, as his boss was caught in a mindset.

"You called it a titan killer? Why?" Gerald asked, the phrase sticking with him ever since his ears heard the claim.

Piper would fell silent, seeing his boss pursuing a query. Abel smiled before answering, smiling as if rapturous just like the Mexicans back at the warehouse, "I believe, should this be poised in the right place, it will strike that bastard dead."

The squeaking of mice to the back of the building could be heard in the absence of words that followed. Gerald was stunned to hear such a claim and struggled in knowing what to do with it. His initial instinct, when faced with such words of audacity, would be to laugh in the speaker's face and follow with a flurry of insults. Another instinct would be a swift departure without a single word being said, utterly insulted by the wasting of his time. But neither actions came and instead what surged was strong consideration, the sincerity in his rival's eyes demonstrating the seriousness. Those eyes would made it believable, and the words, understandable. The logic made sense despite his initial repulsion; to strike a beast in just the right spot. With this consideration, two questions were to spawn in Gerald's mind. He was hesitant to ask at first, reluctant in showing commitment to whatever ludicrous plan Abel had cooped up, but at the same time possessed a strong will to know where this was going.

"Strike him where?" Gerald first asked, sensing no judgement those behind'

"In the name, the brain of course" Abel exclaimed.

Then one last question, "Where do we come into this?"

That anticipated bombshell was now imminent by the look on Abel's face. His rival braced before

74

answering, as if his plan depended on it. "We needed Abijah to make this plan work," Abel said.

Hearing the name of his horseman and friend be spoken by a man he considered venom was ill-received and Gerald arose sharply from his seat.

"Well, Abijah's dead, so there's your plan fucked!" he said with emotion.

"I know he's dead," Abel said as respectfully as he could, "But you have another one."

"Another what?" Gerald sharply asked, his patience wafer thin.

A silence followed, Abel granting Gerald the chance to admit that he knew what his rival was referencing, but Gerald was not to budge.

"You know. Another horseman," Abel said, speaking the answer Gerald already knew.

Gerald sighed loudly before turning to exit the garage, reluctant to hear another word.

"Come on, Gerald!" Abel shouted as he arose from his seat, "Long John is too tall for us to reach his brain, even with his hunch, and we need a horseman that is strong enough to strike!"

Gerald halted just ahead of the door, with Piper closely behind. "He's dead," Gerald's false tongue muttered, the eeriness of the garage carrying the faint words over to Abel.

But Abel was not to be fooled as so many had. "He's not, that's just what you told everyone" he protested. "You see, Leon has done business with you before and casually spilt words concerning a warehouse he sold to you empty upon being bought, but was soon not so he believed. He claimed there was something in there, something big. I had my guys check it out and they found him, Gerald, large as anything. I need you because you are the only one that monster listens to."

Gerald couldn't believe his ears, hearing that his unstable horseman had been found. He shook with shock before planning a foolish flurry of falsehoods, but quickly rendered such efforts useless giving Abel's clear assertiveness. He knew where he was and there was no lying his way out of it. His discarded horseman's involvement made sense in the plan and even made it conceivably possible to achieve, which should have rendered a smile on the face of the man who wanted Long John dead so badly, but the chaos from past involvement of this unruly beast ensured bad memories took primary hold.

Those memories, or more like nightmares, pried from the shadows and to centre stage.

The notorious horseman was Asher Moss, who had served amongst Gerald's ranks up until a decade ago. Measuring over seven feet, Asher towered amongst the others with the strength capable of decimating entire groups of rivals, tearing them limb from limb. But Gerald's reluctance to use Asher did not stem from the horseman's capability, but rather something far more dangerous. Something unfortunate about his character, his unpredictability. Remembering the years of struggle with the beast, Gerald's mind deflated and defeated as he replied, "He doesn't listen to me, he listens to no one."

Abel left the vicinity of the table and approached his rival, stopping several feet behind to attain respect, "But he does, Leon claims he screams your name daily. He's done so for years."

Gerald's wouldn't dare of considering the possibility of freeing his former friend, grew frustrated with the surge of memories, and struck the garage door as a means of venting.

"He's a monster, Abel!" Gerald shouted, "One who caused me so much shit a decade ago!"

Abel then dared to dance closer, stepping further until only two or three paces separated them. "He's hard to tame, I understand, but to kill this monster *we* need a monster, you know this is necessary," he said.

Gerald paused and reflected on the plan that was unfolding, thinking of the faces and the hardships that had been dealt the harshest blows by that horseman, and in the end his safer mind dominated.

"No, I'm not doing it," he said as he shook his head and opened the garage door. Piper followed closely behind as the two exited, the pair eager to evade the situation, but found only mere paces to be taken before a displeased Abel shouted.

Gerald had expected such an outburst and predicted insults, making his decision to denounce the idea even easier. But instead, what sounded was a simple statement of fact, a statement that would resonate with Gerald in a way he didn't predict coming from his fierce rival of all people.

"Then you hand Long John the victory, you fight on as you are and he kills you or you retreat with your cowardice, either way he wins!" Abel proclaimed as he stood at the entrance of the garage.

Such words exploded on Gerald and all previous dominance of his safer and logical mind was decimated, replacing it with a fiercely foolish thought. His rival spoke the truth, he knew — beyond his horseman there was no way to win. And little did Gerald know just how much his rival's words would strike a nerve with his ally.

"For Abijah," Piper said, only loud enough for his boss to hear. Gerald looked to him, seeing the sincerity Piper possessed — he was ready for it if Gerald was.

The decision was made and no words followed, only a stern nod of consent before a sharp turn heading away from the garage.

"I don't like this, boss," protested Fraser as he, Gerald, Piper and numerous members of the Coffin Bearers sat in the carriage heading for a place they had long hoped to forget.

"Neither do I," stressed Gerald to all present, "But this is desperate."

"Yeah, you can say that again," teased an unimpressed Fraser, imitating the feelings of the others.

Gerald saw it in each of them; the looks of fear and anger, but he affirmed his reasoning.

"I know what he's done," Gerald stressed, "And trust me, I don't like it any more than any of you. I saw what he did, the horrors he caused."

The men lowered their heads, respectful to the memories of the besieged, some of them even suppressed tears as their boss grew emotional himself. This syndicate being far more than a firm, but a family.

"But... this bastard... Long John, he took Abijah away from us," Gerald spoke passionately as his posse lifted their heads one by one. "He left his lifeless corpse to rot for rodents, left him in one of those damn displays!"

All men within the carriage now had their heads lifted, and so were their enraged gazes with gritted teeth.

"He took one of our own! Our brother, our blood! And if making this devil pay means seeing Asher's murderous mug again, then so be it!" Gerald roared to emboldened men.

They roared in understanding and chanted words of revenge and bloodshed. But their boss was not to join in the calling, himself falling silent and suppressing the tears as the face of his friend came to mind. A sensational guilt plagued him, for he knew his selfish desire of hunting the beast was of his own making and so was it to drag his horseman with him. Had he not been lustful for such fable, then his friend would still be alive with no need to gaze upon his shameful second horseman.

Piper, knowing his boss' ordeal than any of the men in the carriage, was the only soul to notice his Gerald's anguish and patted his shoulder. "It can't be changed now, boss, but it can be made right!" Piper said, speaking over the chanting. Piper's assurance, the only true piece of its kind, saw Gerald's tears dry and the passion for justice ensue. To hell with the fame, to hell with the money, all he wanted was justice.

Finally, Gerald's chanting carriage arrived at their intended destination, with a carriage carrying Abel and a few of his men arriving just minutes after. Sixteen men in all, half and half. The tension could be cut with a knife, both posses of men giving the stink eye, but both

80

sides had received prior instruction from their leaders to hold their tongues and guns. Each group of men encircled the carriage they had emerged from, none moving until Gerald gave the order. He looked over to Abel at the other carriage, his rival giving a respectable sign of acknowledgement. Abel would know who was in charge of this pursuit, Gerald not moving until he could see it in his eyes. But he would know it after a stern look, ordering them all to move soon after. "Right, let's move!" he shouted to them all, his men and Abel's.

The scenery to await them was dark and dull, fitting for the beast they sought. Even with the moderately-raised sun, the derelict surroundings of the shanty town still granted those unfamiliar, with a shiver and a fright. A couple of men even flinched at the sound of evading mice from amongst debris, fear toying with their composure. Some men, those known to Gerald the longest, had seen the terrible horseman before and were in no rush to revisit him. Others hadn't seen him but were all too aware of the tales ascribed to him, and they perhaps shook the most, for their minds played wonder as to what the beast would appear as. It would be in such a moment, as Gerald looked around to the scared faces surrounding him, that he saw Asher, who had struck fear into the men in similar reverence to Long John. It was clear they saw him as a monster, Abel's words proving truer than ever.

Like entering a cave in search for a ravenous beast the men wasted no time in marching towards their destination, a warehouse that stood at the town's centre — it was of a domineering size to the surrounding buildings. It stood out tremendously and so too did its door, large and heavily-bolted. The warehouse was clearly a marvel of earlier times, the cotton and other fabrics laying waste around its exterior. But despite its clear desolation and age, not a single hole or window was to be seen and thus granted no insight as to what lay within.

"It's strange, he could rip through this door without breaking a sweat and yet he's been here the whole time?" questioned one of Abel's men.

"Gerald commanded it, and so, the beast wouldn't leave," Fraser answered aloud. "You said he was a monster?" queried Abel as he looked at Gerald ahead of him, "Monsters have no masters."

"Asher obeys my order out of sorrow for his actions. He thinks if he listens then one day, I will come back to release him. But I never planned for such a day, never planned for this," Gerald explained.

The look of confusion was seen across many of Abel's men and even among the younger members of Gerald's group, as they were not familiar with the mechanics of the beast.

"He's a monster, but more in the function of a rabid dog," Piper added, "And all dogs need masters, even if they don't listen for the most part, especially when they hit their worst."

"Is this his worst then?" asks Abel as they stood just beyond the bolted door, close enough to hear the horseman's cries. "Indeed, it is," Gerald simply said in defeated tone as the cries become audible. The cries were quick to be accompanied with sounds of banging and smashing, aggressive and horrifying in nature. Cries of: "Gerald, find me!" and: "I'm sorry!" being most prevalent. The sheer velocity of sound forced one of Abel's men to question whether the horseman knew of their presence. "No," Fraser explained, "He's been like this since his incarceration." Fraser looked to his boss, the pair remembering the day they first bolted that door.

The screams of sheer pleas along with the dreaded sounds of expressed regret caused tremendous distress to those unfamiliar, many covered their ears and tried to focus on something else but the anguish was overbearing. The sounds of throwing and smashing, accompanied by screams and grunts, with the cries of regret led some of Abel's men to hastily retreat a few paces. They moved back quickly, with expressions of dismay with even one of them shouting "Holy hell, what did he do?" out of pure panic.

Abel looked ahead to Gerald and Fraser, as if expecting an answer. There wasn't a sole reason to give, Asher's crimes spanning numerous occasions, but Gerald would recite the horseman's final crime that saw him put away. The tip of the proverbial iceberg as it were.

"Remember Guido de Sorbo?" Gerald begrudgingly found himself asking his rival.

"Yes? That guappo, got hung out to dry by your guys over hell knows what and left in a hideous state. Some say it was over drugs, or over money or women. Caused a massive bloodbath, you lost a lot of guys starting a fight with him. I mean, what were you thinking and what did you even want?" Abel responded.

"It wasn't 'guys' that started it, just one," Gerald replied.

Abel would question who, but then noticed his rival staring hauntingly at the warehouse in front, hearing the horseman's cries of apology.

Gerald continued with the dampest expression, "Of all the people he could've unleashed his madness on, it had to be the one with the determined wife. I put him here, told him never to leave, and entrusted Leon to feed him."

"Like a dog?" Abel queried.

"Exactly," Piper said.

Gerald, with hesitation and great reluctance, ordered his men to take out the bolts on the door. They did so with haste, prying the bolts as swiftly as they were able, before jumping back to attain a safe distance. The fear on all the faces present, only intensified with the sudden end to smashing and screaming, even among those who once knew of the beast. Gerald, after a deep inhale of prescribed preparation, slowly approached the door and gently pulled it open. The eeriness of the heavy hinges echoing in all directions, served as a replacement for ill-fated sound. Gerald didn't need to look behind him to know that the others had stepped back even further, leaving him alone in this ordeal. Every inch the door was further pushed granted Gerald only more disbelief, knowing what awaited. Never had he thought such a scenario would unfold.

The darkest interior revealed itself with the near full-opening of the door, the remainder of the sun barely able to penetrate the windowless interior. The absence of light would hardly shield Gerald, nor the others behind him, from the horror of odours the opening door revealed, rotting flesh along with urine and faeces. Gerald could hardly hold down his food upon smelling the savagery, with some men behind compelled to cough and heave. He looked back to those behind as if in need of encouragement to enter, but he would find none of the fearful faces. Even Fraser displayed reluctance, no longer familiar with the beast. With only silence ahead of him, he spoke to himself, "Come on, just do it." Alone and unaided, the army of one entered the pit in search of the gut-wrenching ghoul.

Despite his determination, his legs shook, his knees wavering as if he were ancient. He felt less of the sun on his back with every step further ventured and soon the thick shade was all-consuming, even with the door open and his posse still in view, he felt alone in the seemingly endless black. Every step echoed, filling the entire space, and he felt his feet sinking — he could only dread to think what he was standing in. It wasn't to be a straight walk, as se collided with a host of broken debris. Gerald knew he was amongst the unfortunate objects to be smashed only moments ago. Wood, metal, fabric, glass, all different and yet bearing the same shattered end.

Gerald must have ventured no further than ten paces before considering the path well-travelled, only allowing his words to journey further. "Asher," he said, though nowhere near as loud as needed, the word not so much as echoing despite the pure silence. The men beyond the wide-open door couldn't even hear it. He was reluctant and knew that despite all that had been done getting here, it wasn't too late to turn back and lock the door. But should his name be called; the fateful wheels would firmly turn. Reluctance was normal but given no alternative paths, he was to shun those doubtful voices and shout as was needed. "Asher!" he said but far louder, perhaps louder than necessary. The voice echoing far into the warehouse, Asher's name rebounding a myriad of times.

Silence followed, his heart pounding, knowing there was no retreating now, he looked back with a fearful expression none could see and noticed those awaiting outside had stepped back even further. The sheer pounding of his chest, coupled with the blackest shading, prevented him from knowing of the horseman's approach until he was well within proximity. In what should have been gradually-loudening steps, were instead sudden thuds of the highest intensity. The powerful footsteps creating a pounding sensation that would overwhelm the one in Gerald's chest.

He retreated a couple of paces from natural caution and the powerful footsteps suddenly ceased, the loudest being the last. Gerald assumed that the horseman was right in front of him, feeling the wind contract in the speed, but found himself squinting out of a complete lack of visualisation. There was nothing, by telling of the eyes alone, there would be no difference between him standing one foot away or one thousand. Squinting wouldn't do it and Gerald advanced his swaying his arms ahead, but he felt nothing. He couldn't see or hear anything but Gerald was certain his horseman was ahead. "Are you there?" he asked, every muscle tensing and mind ready.

Silence was to persist but a sudden shock to the eyes would ensure it wouldn't be the case for long.

"Christ!" says Gerald with a complete lack of composure, abruptly stepping back and almost tripping. His outburst echoed greatly and the sounds of gasping could be heard emanating from the men to the distance.

"Asher, don't do that!" Gerald said as he stood only a metre from the horseman, Asher's face just catching the light protruding from the open entrance. The bending horseman tightened the distance further still, not ceasing until mere inches parted them, before the first sign of expression would be known.

"Bo… B… Boss, is that you?" Asher asked, sniffling and damp-eyed.

With persevering reluctance and shame, Gerald spoke to the man he hoped would never darken his eyes again.

"It is," he said with restraint and a clenched-fist, fighting back all that possessed him to scream angrily and retreat, the horseman grabbed Gerald and hoist him from the ground.

"Boss, am I forgiven. Am I boss, really?" he'd say as he squeezed and cradled his judge with a voice of the highest wretchedness, his excitable wails echoing far into the nightmares of those awaiting outside. His voice, echoing naturally as if it were the voice of three men at different ages.

Gerald faced tremendous discomfort as the horseman hugged him, the pain from the mammoth squeezing was intense but would serve as no rival to the pain of speaking the next sentence. It would be one he could never truly feel, made impossible by the past, but he knew there would be no other way.

Asher put him down and Gerald would regain his breath, "You... you are," he said soon after.

Given Asher's unstable emotions, Gerald had braced for a dramatic display of euphoria by stepping back a couple of paces but soon found the action to be unneeded.

The horseman instead rose fully upright, and pointed his face stood beyond the protruding light from the door, and simply said "Freedom and forgiveness... alas."

To hear the ease in his horseman's voice proved uncomfortable for Gerald, the horseman's happiness undeserved in Gerald's mind, and he was quick to announce the condition for this falsely-displayed reunion. "You are forgiven, but on a condition," Gerald said.

"A condition?" questioned the horseman as he leant down once more, "What can such a worthy condition be?"

"I want you to kill someone for me. A monster, a fiend. Do this… and all is forgiven."

Asher growled like a rabid hound as he picked up a sizeable item of hell knows what, saying, "Then they shall be torn to shreds!" as he threw it far into the darkness. It sounded metallic as it shattered like glass. His temper and strength were still present and Gerald was to find relief in knowing this, he would be a suitable adversary for the beast back at Sparks.

Since Gerald's entry into the warehouse, no waiting man were standing as closely as they had beforehand. Many men had taken six or so paces back with the unnerving sounds within and some had even doubled that. But all would know the feeling of wanting to scarper with the highest speed when the emergence of the horseman came.

Gerald emerged first, dirty and odorous, but couldn't announce Asher's arrival before his monstrous proportion met the full rays of the sun. Gasps and a host of inaudible words sounded, likely of shock and of overwhelming sensation. The full and uncensored view of the horseman proved a tough pill for all to swallow, even Gerald, as the sun revealed it whole. Gerald, along with those in his ranks who hadn't seen him for a decade, were shocked to remember the unsettling look. Asher had always been uneasy to the eye but now he would be even worse. His eyes and lips, no longer bronze but black. The skin, no longer of light gold and now a heavily-polluted orange. A jawline too big for the face and a long-abused slickness in the hair, all toppled above the rugged remains of what was a pristine coat.

"These are our allies," Gerald told him. Asher simply nodded as he towered above them, not questioning the members of Helmswood, as he was not accustomed to the rivalry the two groups shared. Abel gave a staunch look as he displayed the Brain Stake in his hand — Gerald looked to him and then his horseman, knowing those wheels were firmly turning.

They marched back into the Sparks borough the following day like men ready for war, and for the first time since the meeting with the Mayor, their rapturous mentality had returned. They were ready and with the horseman along with the Brain Stake, they dared to predict how the day would end. They entered the borough in three carriages; Abel and his men in one, Gerald and his in another and Asher alone in a third. Gerald looked to the men surrounding him and then across to the opening where Asher in the other carriage could be seen. He would grin at the events that were unfolding around him. An army, stronger than any who went before, marching past the skulls of the besieged to end the tyrant's wrath with riches awaiting them.

It was the last image of that fantasy that stuck with him, a vision of much wealth being given to them, but his grin faded. It had only dawned on him now just a how little a role, if any, the financial gain had played in the hunt for Long John. The money of offer was tremendous, more than his syndicate would make in three years, and yet it never plagued him. He wasn't to be concerned with it and, as he thought about it, it appeared he wasn't the only one.

Piper and Abijah never mentioned the money and neither did Abel or any within his ranks. Not even a schilling was mentioned at the garage, where this whole plan's foundation was laid.

Gerald thought back to the Mayor and his words at the start of this chaos: "I know you are here for the money and those who kill him will certainly get it, but I implore you to be motivated by something other than this. You're going to need it if you want to end his reign of terror."

His words would be truer to these men than any others, more than any who've walked this path of death. The faces around him reeked of it, a burning passion of fire different to what was kindled before. This would be why they were alive, Gerald knew, for their passion was to dethrone the king and not to be concerned with the wealth that followed. The money meant nothing, the glory of killing the beast alone was payment enough and would ensure a far longer lasting dynasty than simple coins.

"Boss, you all right?" Piper asked, noticing the look of deep thought on his face.

Gerald broke from contemplation and embraced in an outward and emboldened display. "Are we ready to slay this monster among men?" he shouted.

"Yes!" they all answered. "Then, may history know us as the ones who ended this fiend! To death with Long John!" Gerald roared, the sound of unified war cries emanating immediately after.

The carriages came to pass a certain street corner where Jude was waiting to report. He had been sent there ahead of the others in a bid to locate the fiend before the group's arrival back into the borough. Being Abel's guy, Gerald's rival would leave his carriage to talk with the scout but it soon became clear that there was an issue.

"Uh oh, don't like the look of that," said Piper as he saw Abel kick rubbish from the pathway and heard him shouting expletives.

Gerald huffed as he anticipated a problem and got out of his carriage to join the pair. "Stay put" he said to his guys as he left alone.

"What's the problem?" Gerald queried as he approached Abel and Jude.

"The Hatzi family," Abel simply said. "The Greeks, they've been spotted walking the streets to the south of Sparks. Apparently armed and ready — no need to guess why they're here." Jude explained.

"But, why?" Gerald asked with confusion. "Why now when us lot are still here?"

"That bastard Mayor I reckon," debated Abel, "He must've heard of the Yanks and Mexicans being slaughtered and found the rest of us absent. He's probably entrusting them lot to finish the job. But as if that's going to happen."

"Or they could be hired by someone else," Gerald added, "Either way it doesn't matter, they don't have what we have. Hell, they'll probably be dead by the time we meet the fiend."

"Where is he anyway?" Gerald then asked, knowing of Jude's role as scout.

"A part of the market called Deplin, a back alley that's mostly used for piling waste from the local shops," he answered.

The men re-entered their carriages and headed for the Deplin corner, attempting to get as close as they were able. On route, Gerald explained the arrival of the Greeks to the borough, which was ill-received with a host of angry responses. The Hatzi clan were a fearful bunch whose activities in Thessaloniki would reach ears as far west as London and beyond, ruthless and persistent to say the least. And those of lesser mind would simply express mindless anger at the prospect of the Greeks' involvement, seeing them as nothing more than an inconvenience. Gerald had displayed such a mindset in the presence of his rival and had even joked of the Greeks' premature deaths, but in the carriage, he adopted a different tone. He was cautious of them, very cautious and warned his men to watch out for the group's potential presence. It was true the group didn't possess a horseman or a weapon like the Brain Stake, so they believed, but the group's reputation for the unlikeliest victories made them an adversary to be wary of.

Eventually, the cavalry of carriages made it as close to Deplin corner as was possible, and finish the journey on foot through the heavily-crowded market just ahead of them. Only Jude knew this part of the borough and so he led the convoy with the rest of them following in close pursuit. Fraser was instructed by Gerald to walk at the back of the group to stay with Asher, him being amongst the most able to cope with him.

The horseman had been strangely silent throughout the journey and only spoke for the first time in the present moment, "How will I know who he is?" Asher asked in a voice that strangely suggested hesitation.

"You'll know, trust me," Fraser answered, himself nervous.

Like Asher, Fraser had never set eyes on Long John but his mind had envisioned a hideous view in preparation, using a description provided by Gerald earlier on. The horseman would never voice it, likely not knowing how to even describe such an abnormal feeling, but he too was frightened. He knew the target who needed to be besieged must've been one of mammoth lethality, otherwise, why would Gerald require him?

Gasps could be heard all around the determined convoy as the market goers gazed upon the towering size of Asher, "Strange, one would think these people would be used to such an abnormal sighting. With Long John being here and all," Piper said.

"Long John is a monstrosity many here grew up with, Asher is not," Gerald replied.

"Well, they will soon know his name and appearance for the rest of their lives after today — his and all of ours," said Abel with high optimism, hearing them talk closely behind him.

The gazes only multiplied as the convoy soon found themselves at the centre of the market, their attire and weapons made them easily identifiable and thus the looks grew sterner.

"I don't like this, there's too many eyes on us!" said a concerned Fraser.

"It's fine, they're just looking at Asher that's all," replied Gerald untruthfully.

"No, it's definitely all of us," Piper protested.

"It's fine!" said a nervous Abel abruptly. "Jude, how much further?"

"Not far" he insisted, himself growing nervous.

The crowd grew tighter with sterner faces, each onlooker expressing no desire to move and so harsh barging soon followed. None would voice it but the convoy of near twenty would be unified in the tremendous feeling of unease, a notion they had prepared for with the monster but not from these people. Women and children acted just as boldly and had to be forcibly shoved aside in order to pass. The atmosphere was quickly advancing into something hideous and, with his rival yet to advise anything, Gerald took it upon himself to lead.

"Draw your weapons," Gerald muttered to all within earshot, with the instruction being passed to the others, even within Abel's ranks. There would be no dispute and they all reached for their concealed weapons, but upon doing so the mass of people ahead halted entirely and formed a blockade as if seeing the hunters' actions coming.

"Step aside, now!" shouted a furious Abel as their weapons were revealed and raised.

"We will fire!" added Gerald.

A sharp silence ensued for a moment as the raised weapons laid aim at the mob ahead, refusing to budge. They were just everyday market goers, fearless ones at that once their determination was to be known. A multitude of seconds would pass and they clearly possessed no intentions of moving, their faces remaining ever stern and eyes rarely blinking.

"You think I'm messing around?" said Abel as he shoved his pistol into one of the people's cheeks, veins pulsing with frustration at the inconvenience. But the fearless expressions of the crowd persisted.

They were in a standoff and the convoy found themselves in a restrained situation. Causing a bloodbath before they had even reached Long John was hardly ideal. Not to mention, they needed every man they had. Killing them was not in their interest but clearly a harsh response was needed to punch a hole through this wall of fanatics.

"I'm going to count to three," said Abel as he cocked his weapon.

The people remained undeterred.

"Three… two… one," he said. Abel was about to pull the trigger to cease a middle-aged gent ahead of him but stopped as a man from within the crowd pushed himself to the front. He was the first and only member of this mob to speak, such actions halting Abel in his tracks.

"We will not let you go against him!" said the emerging man loudly and with determination, "People like you... you just make things worse. His temper, it gets worse when your kind come, and innocents die. We know where you're going and we will not let you pass!"

Shocked and confused, Gerald walked up to the man and asked, "Why do you protect a monster? You speak of him as if he's one of you."

"A monster to you but not us!" the man protested with nodding heads all around him, "He's not perfect, but without him your poison would run rabid on these streets. Just like you've done everywhere else in this cursed city, hell, if we live under the same tyranny!"

The crowd became ever more emboldened by such words and voices their own praises in the aftermath. "Since that blessed Christmas decades ago, he's protected us!" shouted one.

"Angel, not a monster!" said another.

Many of the convoy sigh openly in reaction to the bizarre words of affection to the fiend, some laughing and others shouting cusses. But a member of the convoy wasn't to indulge in the war of words unfolding and rather shouted to his boss at the front.

"Should I kill them, boss?" said Asher. The warring ceased upon the sound of the horseman's voice, loud and transparent.

The silence returned and with it, but Gerald was to reproach with a different argument.

"We were asked to come by invitation of your Mayor, a grieving father who saw his daughter in a way no man should. I do not care how you view him, we have a job to do. Now out of our way!" he shouted.

That was not his motive, nor was it of any within the convoy, they wanted his fame but tried to display finesse in their reasoning. The people still refused to move which prompted a final warning from a man who saw no other option. "We will kill everyone here if we have to, now move!" said Abel with the highest aggression.

All other men cocked their guns at this point, including Gerald with his Silver Death, and awaited the first strike. It was to come imminently as Abel's finger was beginning to press against the trigger, but was to unexpectedly stop with the sounding of yet another voice. This one from behind them.

"Let them through!" shouted a man. The convoy turned around to see a crowd of near equal size behind them.

"Let them through, this madness has to end," the man reiterated.

The convoy no longer found themselves on one side of the simple black and white divide, but were now sandwiched between opposing colours. The social divide concerning the beast, clear for all to see.

"I can't do that, Hector, these men can't be allowed to bring out the worst in our angel. It will only intensify his temper and cause havoc for the rest of us," argued the man.

"Enoch, this is madness. Your own son fell foul to his temper and yet you stand there and defend that monster? There will be no punishment for us as these men will kill him, look at their horseman — he's the one that will do it," argued the man identified as Hector.

"What makes this one so special when two horsemen have died already in this wave alone?" said the one referred to as Enoch. "And don't you dare bring up my boy, he was struck because damn bastards like these aggravated him! They are not passing and that's final!"

"Fine, have it your way," muttered Abel.

Abel's gun was poised once more, certainly the last time before blood would spill. Gerald knew such looks in a man and saw no alternative to what was to follow. The wheels were set in motion and there would be nothing he could do, but he looked back just before the bullets started to rain down and saw Hector and the supporting crowd behind.

An unfortunate but assertive nod, knowing no other way. Abel would lead the slaughter, his bullet penetrating the naïve Enoch's skull, acting as only a drop for the shower to follow.

All other guns sounded and the opposers were levelled, no longer a soul in front of them. No screams from any non-participants sounded, no strangers to bloody ends, and only the echoes followed. The smell of blood was strong in the air and many fresh corpses laid beneath their feet, a horrid sight but necessary nonetheless.

Gerald looked behind him towards the other group. "Kill him," mimed a saddened Hector.

Gerald nodded just as Abel ordered the convoy to advance. They did so and stepped over the many corpses on the way.

They would face no further disruption on route to their designation and soon only inches separated them from Deplin corner.

"The time is upon us!" Gerald rallied, "Long John will see his end on this very day, and we will be the ones to lay privilege to the claim!"

Such outward displays of fearlessness were well-received by men from both groups and they replied with roars. Gerald was a changed man; no more did he fear over the fiend's image. His knees no longer weary like before, now springier with every nearing step. Gerald embraced the moment and gazed at the cascade of souls around him. To his devoted men; Piper and the likes. Then to his rivals; Abel and his ilk. And finally, to the horseman; displaying an unusual calmness for the first time. The latter would stick with him.

Seeing his horseman so calm and measured for the first time served testimony to what awaited, or so he thought, with Gerald believing it stemmed from a readiness to slay the beast. But not even the horseman would know his own mind, himself unfamiliar with the actual reasoning for his perceived calmness. Not calm, but silent. Silent in fearful anticipation.

Like David to Goliath, Spartans to the Persians, Crusaders to the Saracens, and Vandals to the Byzantines, the mortal men marched to the formidable foe, awaiting the fight that saw history reserve their names.

"Remember, Asher, plunge it into the bastard's head and it's over," reminded Gerald as the corner came into view.

Asher nodded with certainty, his inner panic unseen. The convoy's confident and wide strides grew smaller and cautious as the corner faced right in front of them, their bodies were tensed and guns ready as they prepared for the fateful encounter that awaited them just around the other side.

"This is it," whispered Piper to his boss, Gerald breathing deeply as they prepare to turn. With tremendous swift and haste, the convoy of gunslingers turned the corner onto the back alley behind with weapons raised and aggressive gazes. Asher was slow to move and had developed a shaking sensation upon turning, which no one noticed in the commotion, but all would be proven useless once the contents awaiting were known.

Hearts of adrenaline would dampen with frustrated minds to swiftly follow as only the back of the shops filled their view.

"Jude, what the hell? You want to explain something to me?" Abel demanded to know as he grabbed his chap by the coat.

"No, boss, I swear, this is where he was last sighted. He hasn't been seen anywhere else," swore a desperate Jude.

"Well, he's obviously not here!" shouted Gerald, whose frustration was equally clear, "Trust this to be fucked up by one of your guys!" he teased.

Abel's frustration with Jude was suddenly directed towards Gerald for his comment. "And what the fuck do you mean by that?" Abel asked as he approached Gerald aggressively.

Gerald would return the aggressive approach by marching towards him, at which Piper jumped to intervene.

"Stop, this won't help!" Piper insisted, not wanting this truce to expire abruptly, but it didn't prevent the two leaders from minor squabbles as the pair engaged in pushing. Some from either rank joined in as a consequence, shoving and poorly-swayed punches commencing. But not all were to engage; others preventing and some doing nothing. Benjamin from Abel's group saw no interest in the bloodless squabbles unfolding around him as he, like all present, was frustrated and disappointed about the fruitless find, but he saw fists as no substitute for the disappointment. Benjamin sat on a rickety-stall beside the heap of trash and watch with no motivation to join in.

The squabbles persisted and punches grew bolder, though the guns remained concealed. Benjamin sighed as the events unfolded, a cascade of pointless limbs striking in all directions. But amongst it all, he was to notice how one particular member was reacting to the scene. The horseman, standing as stiffly as stone. Benjamin, hearing of the temper this Asher possessed, was surprised to view such a sight and questioned to himself why. He heard the words from beyond the garage door only a few days ago, remembering how the horseman was described as a monster and hard to tame.

And yet here he was; the most measured of them all. He found the stance odd, how the horseman just wavered there above the flurry of fists, but a certain feature disturbed him.

Those eyes, were not frozen but fixated. The horseman was focussing on something and the realisation led the curious Benjamin to follow the glimmering of his gaze. It led straight past him and to the right. The following of those eyes led Benjamin to turn and look behind to the back ends of the row of shops. Nothing special, just closed doors with empty windows high above them. Benjamin thought nothing of it and disappointedly turned back around to face the bruising horde, putting it down to just strange behaviour of a man he wasn't familiar with. He tutted in the moment and looked at the horseman.

"What are you looking at?" the raising of an eyebrow would suggest. Growing irritated and uncomfortable.

But Asher's eyes didn't know of Benjamin for they were too fixed on the back ends of the shops and one door in particular. Benjamin saw the horseman's eyes widen to a hideous degree and a creaking sound followed.

The others were too busy squabbling to notice as the fearful Benjamin slowly turned his head to the doors, he had viewed just seconds before. Benjamin saw the cause of Asher's fixation and, froze with fear. Benjamin remained still, his racing heart consuming him entirely. The door widened until it could creak no more and the petty crowd was still yet to notice.

Benjamin wanted to vomit from the surreal unearthing, the way those arms twisted out of the door and limbs unfolded from the tight space was sickening. With every part that escaped the tight confinement of the shop like the foulest birth, those limbs unravelled and he was standing with abnormal height once more. It was only then, when he was standing proudly with his arch and cane, that one of the squabblers noticed, and the reason spread like the plague.

There he stood, the soul they had come to claim, and yet not a body was to move. Every heart, pounding in unison. They had marched with fabled desire and now stood as homeless mutts with quivering legs. Long John commenced in a single stride towards Benjamin, the nearest of them all, bending down to glare at him deeply. His instinct for higher breath was all that echoed in the moment whilst the others watched as if unarmed. The petrified Benjamin shook, as if winter had made a swift return and rendered him nude.

The awaiting grey above fittingly spit its harsh rains in that moment, the contents quickly filling the flurry of craters in the uneven ground. The rain was vibrant and battered against the many materials that wasted in the heap of rubbish, creating loud patters and yet the pure tremble in Benjamin sounded louder.

Gerald couldn't believe what was unfolding, an unwelcomed guest's return. He felt the inferiority for the second time but in no parallel to the first, where he laid eyes on the fiend only nights ago. No, this felt far worse, seeing his terrified stature be replicated amongst all around him, including Asher. It was how the horseman reacted that would seal everyone's fate.

The feared fable ripped Benjamin from reality right before their very eyes, the entrails infecting every brick of the alley. No one moved in the immediate aftermath, the overwhelmed faces remaining along a sudden plea for a quick death.

Gerald shed a tear in the moment, the drop descending and mixing with the splatter of fresh blood from Benjamin's slaughter, and dared to gaze at the Silver Death in his light grasp. His arm rose, shaking, the gun cocked, he fired — starting a battle that had already ended.

Just like that fateful night, the bullet bounced straight off the monster, the shell landing beside Abel's foot. Gasps followed. None could believe their eyes beside Gerald, who thoughtlessly prepared for a second shot. He fired just as the rain intensified, and again the bullet bounced. He prepared a third, but a shot sounded before he fired, this one being taken by his rival.

Abel roared in readiness for the next shot, his actions were infectious and all everyone fired with a war cry. The sounds of screaming, shooting and following bloodshed would echo across the entire borough, adding fame to the fable as all who heard knew of its meaning. Hector lowering his head, regretting his actions in voicing favour to the convoy, now wishing they had walked away.

The sky darkened and the rain persisted, and as the echoes of screams and bullets faded, a lone man walked the deserted markets. Battered and bruised, bleeding from the mouth and ears, he left a trail of blood behind him, dripping and mixing in the many puddles. His breathing sang out of sync with the patters of rain and his ribs crunching, his body taking a tremendous toll. His face was soaked in the breezing rain and yet he could tell there were tears. His physical pain was horrendous but his mental would be worse. Knowing the slaughter ha had seen, the reluctant flashbacks emanating more pain than his body ever could. He tried to evade them, shaking his head sharply as the images came and would utter cusses in regret but they couldn't be prevented.

Every limb torn, drop spilt, and lifeless body lay, he remembered them all. The images forever sealed in a vault that should always be empty. The bullets fired matched the number of drops from the sky but despite their uselessness, they pursued anyway. Amongst the chaos the frozen horseman finally melted and moved, rushing to blindly strike the fiend with the Brain Stake. The cleanest angle to the head and it bent, his skull entirely intact. None would register, as the bullets continued, for they would all know the truth in the fables to this beast. Retreat would be no desire for any of them, preferring the fable of death by monster than no fable at all. Asher wasn't able to take a single step in reverse after the fateful attempt, losing his head in time too small to name, and others would soon follow in butchered ends. Gerald would find himself struck and launched into the heap of the rubbish to the side, going black for a time before awaking to see the sight that now haunts him.

They were left as they were killed, not even deemed worthy enough by the fiend for one of his displays.

A defeated man, both in body and soul, walked those eerie streets and would trip on something beyond sight. He fell and landed on his front, none around to see and none around to help.

Gerald would cry though not from the fall, itself only serving as the tip of the proverbial iceberg. Despite his grave loss he wouldn't weep for himself but for those who couldn't. A flurry of faces would draw him and tears would flow for each; for his dear friend Piper, for Abijah, for Fraser, for Asher and strangely even for

Abel and all in-between. Crying for his rival would lead his emotional state to weep for all those who had died in this battle, present and past. Different they all were, but the same in goal. They were unified in motive but Gerald would stand alone in this feeling for no man had ever walked away from the fiend's battering.

He looked up to the sky and screamed as loudly as his throat would allow, the chords tearing from the strain. No words, only sound, dreadful sound. That would be a sound none of the inhabitants of the borough would know. The besieged man would scream in waves, not ceasing until his voice forced him to. He would curl up on the ground amongst the mud and crap like a lost child, folding his arms around his legs and rocking lightly. He stayed there for a while, rocking away and wishing for it all to stop, before a glimmering from the breaking lunar rays above penetrated his darkened eyes.

They opened to see an object a few metres beyond him, he had a hunch as to what it was but he had to feel his side to be certain. It was his Silver Death, likely departing from his person upon the fall. His mind would grant his wish for the end to come and so he pulled his carcass across the harsh and soaked landscape. With every pull came more tears, tears that came with the images of the besieged and teasing of what could've been. If only that stake had pierced him, he tortured himself, how different the world would've been. They could've triumphantly dragged the corpse through the streets, parading it on route to the Mayor. They would receive the loot but, far more importantly, the reputation that would last far beyond their bodies. But not to be and instead he would find himself dragging through mud and crap, intending on ending the torture.

With one foul reach, Gerald extended for the gun once he was close enough and gripped onto it tightly. He arose, preferring to die on the feet than on his knees, his arm shaking as he rose it to his temple. The tears ceased as he rose, his mind blank as the fateful moment came. Eyes closed, teeth tensed, gun cocked. Symbolically, one round in the chamber, one more life to end this mad dream. He was to fire but found the most abrupt sound frustratingly stopping him. It proved so overwhelming, he jolted and dropped his Silver Death.

Gerald shook, and breathing erratically, though not from the loudest of sounds, but rather the breaking of readied state. That was his courage and he was unlikely to build it back. Frustrated, he picked up his gun and marched in the direction of the sound's eminence.

"What the hell was that?" he wondered. "It sounded like an explosion."

A bewildering bang like that would echo for many miles, making it hard to guess just how close one was to the sound's origin, but Gerald was quick to see just how close he was by the view of brazen embers burning upwards to the near distance. He was angry that such a moment, one that could never be done so thoughtlessly again, had been stolen from him. Stolen by the sound. That, along with the pent-up disappointment of defeat.

The turning of only a small number of streets and alleys to get to the source revealed no more than a couple evading souls, the time being late with the streets being almost completely empty. He ran past them, and ignoring one of their pleas for him to turn back, he ran faster towards the sound of gunfire. There were so many shots, too many at once to be from a single man and so he approached with caution, intrigued as well as angry. The sight he beheld rendered him to halt sharply, almost falling in the process, the view being far from what he expected.

In what he initially believed to be a simple robbery of some kind, then thinking it was a gunfight between rivals, were both proven to be incorrect with the view far surpassing what he could've conjured from mere sounds. He was shocked and surprised but it would bring him no pleasure or hope, knowing that beast could not be ended. He knew it was pointless, but how where those Sikhs to know? They were only facing him for the first time.

Their efforts were commendable and their planning impressive as the fiend lay crushed beneath a collapsed bridge that had clearly been blown up with explosives.

Balteg and his goons fired endlessly at the face of the fiend, it being all that protruded from the rubble, only taking breaks to reload.

Gerald watched the cycle repeat three times before he made his presence known, and walked over to them and utter the words of the locals. A notion he had never seen coming, where he proclaimed the fable to strangers.

"There's no point, it's useless," Gerald said as the men ceased firing and pointed their guns towards him.

"He can't be killed!" Gerald continued, walking up to the fiend, showing no fear of the guns being pointed at him. He passed them and stood before Long John amongst the fire and debris.

"He can't be killed," he'd say once, only this time with more sincerity.

He wouldn't blink as he gazed into the eyes of the monster who had taken so much away from him, those dead and warped eyes gazing straight back. One would think that after all this beast had stolen from him, there'd be resentment and anger. But there wasn't and what stood in their place was something far more powerful. It was something he would be second to know in this wave of hopefuls, a certain horseman finding it first. It was the horseman's swiftness in knowing it that enabled him to leave intact when so many others didn't.

Acceptance. Acceptance in knowing the stories of this beast were true; unkillable, and a monster amongst men.

As Gerald displayed such a look, Balteg's goons laughed at Gerald's claims, seeing him as a victim to the stories, but Balteg himself took offence. He promptly took aim at the beast once more, saying, "Anything is killable." before shooting a flurry of bullets. All of them, equally as useless as the last, with not one to seed.

"I speak the truth," said Gerald as he stared Balteg in the eye, "And you know it."

Balteg could never admit it, but he knew of the truth in Gerald's words, his eyes deeming it irrefutable. But the realisation of his pride being ridiculed by others, along with the frustration of his inferiority, led the proud Sikh to strike Gerald to the ground with the butt of his pistol — Gerald's own flying far beyond view in the struggle.

"Coward!" he shouted, secretly knowing Gerald was not. His goons stopped their laughing and joined their boss in pointing muzzles towards the bleeding Gerald.

"There's no place for them!" Balteg shouted as he cocked his weapon.

"No place for pride," Gerald whispered.

Gerald, surrounded by the means of an end by which he desired only moments ago, closed his eyes to accept what was coming, his body curled into a ball, awaiting those fateful shots. They came, and whilst his life should've been taken, only his would be the one to stay.

Unexpectedly, the bruised Gerald opened his eyes once more, becoming quickly aware of the strange scenario unfolding around him. Balteg and his goons lay lifeless and bloody as they surrounded him from the ground. Gerald couldn't believe it and lifted his head up with haste to view the cause of this selfish saving. Who would save him? he wondered, not having any allies left. His eyes would lay upon them, a sizeable group of heavy arms, but wouldn't know their faces. Even with the aid of the embers, they stood just beyond affirmative view and so couldn't know them. But the two simple words emerging from the figure closest would render it obvious, the accent unmistakable.

"Such foolishness," the voice said in Greek tone and with it, Gerald wished the Raj had fired.

Unarmed, the helpless Gerald froze as the group in their entirety emerged within full view of the burning embers. Their guns all pointing straight towards him as they shortened the distance. Most stopped at a certain point but three continued until they stood no more than two metres from Gerald. He couldn't be certain, never having put faces to the group before, but Gerald assumed the identities of those standing closest. The leaders, siblings in all. Jace, Hera and Adrian, he would guess.

"Damn Greeks!" Gerald told himself, frustrated that they should be the last ones standing. But he'd take comfort from knowing their journey was a wasted one. Gerald laughed at them in a display of disrespect. "You're the foolish ones, you won't kill him. You can't!" teased.

They didn't answer, the brothers maintaining a fearless gaze at Gerald whilst the sister received an item from a lesser member of the group. This item caused Gerald's humour to cease abruptly.

"Hey, that's mine!" he shouted.

Hera inspected the Silver Death, viewing it from multiple angles before gifting it to her brother.

"Here, Jace," she said.

Jace held the weapon and also inspect it but with distaste.

"Many I have seen like this," he tutted.

Gerald laughed at the insult. "That is a rare piece, the rarest Derringer you'll ever find!" he said.

"Not that." Jace tutted again, shaking his head. "But what they mean... special... but not so. As if they are meant for special killings."

Jace then spat on it and Gerald, repulsed and infuriated, attempted to rise and strike.

He was quickly met with a right-hand from Adrian and a close-up with Hera's muzzle.

"If you're going to kill me, then do it!" he demanded, "Hell knows why you haven't already."

Hera's muzzle then retracted its closeness and Jace clicked his fingers. At once, his siblings rushed for Gerald, turned him around and hoisted him partially upright, facing towards the overwhelmed Long John who had been waiting motionless beneath the rubble. That expressionless face, still there now and forever, Gerald believed.

"We want to show you something," Jace said.

"Yeah?" queried a bewildered Gerald, "And what the hell is that?"

Adrian released his grip from Gerald's right arm and Jace came to replace him, the brother then approaching the soulless fiend. Gerald watched as Adrian walked within inches of the fiend, whose lifeless gaze stared up towards him.

"What the hell is he doing?" Gerald asked himself, "What are they expecting from this?"

The brother, Adrian, reached for his ears and shuffle the tips of his index fingers within them, Gerald's forced stare turned into fixation as he wondered what on earth was unfolding. After a moment, Adrian unearthed firm balls of fine cotton from either ear, the toughness of the emersion suggesting the sheer depth of their embedment. Adrian raised an arm with the gun in his hand, and Gerald sighed over the pointless prospect — just as he had with the Sikhs. He found the scenario ridiculous, how the brother waved so brazenly a standard Percussion Revolver against the centre of the beast's head. A monster, which he knew from experience, could not be killed. He voiced this in the form of laughter, attempting to belittle the shooter in front of his family and followers, but Gerald would be an audience of one. Entirely unaware of his own foolishness, Gerald screamed in utter disbelief with the shot that came. The sound echoing far beyond the realms, none heeding it as they laid in their beds — seeing it as yet another bullet, not aware it was to be the last.

Gerald's eyes flooded in despair and insult as they gazed upon him, the fiend's gaze now truly lifeless. The blood, just like from any man, pouring from the entry wound as Adrian reaped the fabled riches.

"How... how is that... possible?" Gerald cried, hardly suspending vomit. Jace on his right would hold Gerald's head tightly, ensuring he looked at Long John's corpse and nothing else.

"Take away all the legends, the stories and the myths and all that's left is a man. Only when one realises that, he can kill anything," Jace lightly said, as Adrian placed the cotton back into his ears. "The stories are plagues, affecting all those who hear them. One must separate themselves from it all or die in the madness. People are prone to this, it's in our nature, and now a new plague will come and with a new origin." Jace and Hera unhanded Gerald, stepping back as Adrian stood before him.

His ears were as bewildered as his eyes, neither could believe what they had been exposed to, and Gerald was left in a state of the highest frustration. So many questions ravaged him, with theories and speculations running wild like flames in a dry forest. They all fought for the mouth and in the end, just the simplest would surface. "What do you mean?" he asked, his hands trembling and eyes twitching. Gerald stared up to the emotionless Adrian, tearful and bowing as if a frightened servant to a new master.

Jace handed Gerald his Silver Death, "Use it." he said.

Gerald looked at Jace, utterly perplexed at such an opportunity, did the idiot not doubt his actions?

Jace return no such blankness but rather the purest certainty, predicting the action to come. And so, Gerald found himself amongst the myriad of eyes, all knowing the coming action except him. He looked up to the voiceless Adrian, physically slim and inferior, yet able to make a mockery of the fierce men who had been laid waste only streets away. What he had done was beyond the bewildered Gerald and it made him angry, not justly but jealously. His grip tightened on his gun and he pointed it at Adrian with no objection from the ranks behind. He would shoot with that last bullet, the final attempt to seal some kind of legacy, and yet he couldn't even achieve that. The bullet bounced off the waiting Adrian, as if he were a fiend himself, and Gerald knew of a new plague and would be its first mortal victim. Simply unable to see his opponent as a man after what he had witnessed. Jace's earlier were true — of how believing in such things were in man's nature. What they cannot comprehend will be separated from mortality and rendered higher.

"Just a man," Jace said. "A man you can't see."

Gerald shook profusely, dropped his Silver Death and curled into a ball as before. He closed his eyes, bracing for what was to come. A bang would sound, the shot echoing beyond the realm once more, only this time his eyes weren't to open.